LOVE

Bobbie dressed in her Bubbles the Clown outfit, applied her greasepaint, and then waited for Jay to pick her up. A thousand butterflies danced in her stomach. It wasn't the thought of playing the clown that made her nervous; it was the thought of seeing Jay again. She wanted him to like her, but how could he get to know Bobbie Reese if he only saw her bundled in the clown outfit, her face hidden under tons of makeup. Would Jay like her if he saw the real Bobbie?

Bantam Sweet Dreams Romances
Ask your bookseller for the books you have missed

Love in the Wings

Virginia Smiley

BANTAM BOOKS

TORONTO · NEW YORK · LONDON · SYDNEY · AUCKLAND

RL 6, IL age 11 and up

LOVE IN THE WINGS
A Bantam Book/November 1987

ISBN 0-553-26481-8

Published simultaneously in the United States and Canada

Bantam Books are published by Bantam Books, Inc. Its trademark, consisting of the words "Bantam Books" and the portrayal of a rooster, is Registered in U.S. Patent and Trademark Office and in other countries. Marca Registrada. Bantam Books, Inc., 666 Fifth Avenue, New York, New York 10103.

Printed and bound in Great Britain by
Cox & Wyman Ltd., Reading

O   0 9 8 7 6 5 4 3 2 1

To
Rob
my right hand

Chapter One

"A clown?" Bobbie Reese faced her sister on the front porch of her white colonial-style home. "You have to be kidding!" A cutting January wind blew through her long brown hair. Holding back a shiver, she pulled up the collar of her blue quilted jacket. "You came all the way over here to ask me to make a complete fool of myself?"

Ellen Wilson shrugged her slender shoulders. "I think it's a terrific idea. Let's go inside and talk about it. It's freezing out here." She hugged her fur jacket around her.

Bobbie scowled and shook her head. "It's not that cold. Besides there's nothing to talk about. I won't do it, and that's that." She sat on the porch railing, refusing to acknowledge the fact that her ears were beginning to feel numb. What Ellen was asking was unreasonable. "I told you I'd help with the games for Amy's party tomorrow afternoon, and I will," she said calmly. "But I refuse to put on a ridiculous clown outfit and paint my face. The answer is no. *N-O*."

Ellen drew in a deep breath. "Bobbie, don't you remember how Dad used to make us laugh when he dressed in that funny clown outfit on our birthdays and would try to juggle apples and oranges?"

"The one with the bright green hair? How could I forget!"

Ellen nodded. "That's what I mean. We'll always remember those times." She drew her collar up. "Sure you don't want to go inside?"

"I'm sure."

"You know," Ellen continued, "I bet that costume is still in the trunk in the attic. I remember Dad wore it for a Halloween party a couple of years ago. He had to run out at the last moment to buy a makeup kit. Everything should still be up there. Mom never throws anything away."

"Well, maybe she ought to," Bobbie said, doing her best to remain unapproachable.

Her sister was not put off. "Just think about it. Amy would love it, and—to be honest, I'm not sure a few games will keep ten kids amused for three hours."

Bobbie glared at Ellen. "I thought you said you hired a banjo player."

Ellen nodded. "Yes, a boy named Jay Hartwell. I think he goes to East High. He'll be there, but who knows if these kids will even like banjo music?" She hugged her jacket tighter and decided to try one last time. "A clown would be special, Bobbie. We're talking about five-year-olds. They love crazy faces and corny jokes. Please say you'll do it."

Bobby felt herself weaken. She was crazy about her little niece and did want her birthday party to be a success. Besides, she was getting tired of standing around in the cold, arguing. "All right," she said with a sigh. "I'll look for the costume and see if I can make it work."

Ellen planted a kiss on her sister's cold forehead. "Thanks, Bobbie. You're the greatest!"

Bobbie shrugged. "How can I turn down my only niece?"

"I knew you'd come around. I'm just glad you did it before we both froze to death." Ellen hurried down the driveway toward her car. "I'll pick you up around one tomorrow," she called.

Bobbie watched until the green Chevrolet turned the corner. Then, with a shiver, she went into the house, hung her jacket in the closet, and hurried up the stairs.

The attic door opened off the end of the upstairs hall. It had once been Bobbie's favorite place to play, especially on stormy summer days when the rain beat a steady rhythm on the roof. Now, the big room seemed dreary and smelled of dust.

Bobbie made her way through stacks of *National Geographic* magazines, the kitchen chairs from their last house, discarded toys, and boxes of clothing marked for a charity drive. Hidden behind summer camping gear was the big wooden trunk where her mother stored the sentimental odds and ends that no one else would have kept. She opened the trunk gingerly, half-afraid of what she'd find. The last time she had ventured into its depths, she discovered a report she had written in the fourth grade, embarrassingly titled, "Why We Need Good Manners."

Luckily, it was the clown outfit that caught her eye as the lid creaked open. Bobbie smiled, holding the baggy one-piece outfit in front of her. It had a bright yellow top, a wide, red ruffled collar, and gigantic green pants. Large red buttons ran down the front of the costume. She chuckled, remembering how the thick cotton padding around the waist had made her father look absurdly round. Excited now, she searched for the bushy wig. Folded neatly beside a box of lace doilies lay a mass of light green curls. *It's even sillier than I remembered,* she thought as she plunked it on her head. She dug deeper in the trunk and pulled out a pair of long, floppy black-and-white shoes and the box of grease-paint her father used to complete his disguise. Memories came rushing back—all those parties where she and Ellen had laughed until their sides ached.

Bobbie jumped to her feet, tucking the clown suit under her chin. She danced over to a dressmaker's dummy and bowed low.

"Hi," she chirped, mimicking the high voice her father had used. "I'm Bubbles. I chase away troubles." The sound of her own laughter seemed loud in the big attic.

Well, it might look a little goofy, but she was sure Amy would love it. Actually, she reasoned, it might be fun to be onstage playing the clown this one time. It would only be a couple of hours. She could certainly manage that for Amy. With a final bow to the dummy, she picked up the box of makeup, gathered up the costume, wig, and shoes, and headed for her room.

In the kitchen Mrs. Reese put on the pot of soup that Bobbie had prepared earlier.

"Hi, honey," she called as her daughter came downstairs.

"Hey, Mom. How was your day?" Mrs. Reese worked as a dental technician.

"Quiet. But the weather's getting exciting. The wind's up, and it's starting to snow."

"I sure hope it's nice for Amy's party tomorrow," Bobbie said. "Mom, do you remember Dad's clown outfit?" Her mother nodded. "Well, Ellen seems to think that Amy's party could use a clown, and I've been elected to do the honors. The problem is, I tried on the costume, and I trip over the pants."

Mrs. Reese laughed. "And you would like me to shorten the legs to fit. Am I right?"

A grin spread across Bobbie's face. "I hate to ask. I know you're tired after working all day. I'd shorten them myself, but you know my sewing."

"Yes, I seem to recall a few of your needle-work disasters," Mrs. Reese said, looking amused. "I'll do it later while I watch TV."

"Thanks, Mom," Bobbie said, ladling out two bowls of steaming soup. She was about to fill a third.

"Your father's going to be late tonight," her mother said. "We'll save him some dinner."

"Oh, no," Bobbie moaned. "I was hoping to borrow a clown routine from him."

That night Bobbie dreamed of green-haired

clowns and laughing children. When she awoke on Saturday morning, the grandfather clock in the hall was striking ten. *It's Amy day*, Bobbie thought, as she slid out of bed and crossed the room to the windows. The snow from the night before had stopped, giving way to clear skies and bright sun. Bobbie looked at the glittering trees and hugged herself; she couldn't put her finger on it, but there was something special about that day. In the meantime, though, she had a lot of work to do before Ellen arrived. She wanted her makeup to be perfect, and she needed to pack a few props to use in her act. Then there was the matter of the act itself—she needed some inspiration and fast!

When Bobbie went downstairs for breakfast at ten-thirty she found that her parents had already left, her mother to do some errands and her father to his drugstore. The shortened clown outfit, freshly washed and pressed, was hanging on the kitchen door. Propped up against a plate of homemade blueberry muffins was a note in her mother's neat script:

Good luck with your debut as the green-haired clown. Wish we could be there to laugh with the kids. Give Amy a hug from

Grandma and Grandpa. Fresh o.j. in the frig.

Love,
Mom and Dad

She tucked the note in the back pocket of her jeans, helped herself to a tall glass of orange juice and a muffin, and stood staring at the bright costume. Briefly, she wished her best friend, Nancy, weren't taking a piano lesson that afternoon. Nancy would never believe what she was about to do. In fact, she wasn't sure *she* believed it. Mentally, she reviewed some of her father's better-known routines and tried to picture herself as the clown.

Bobbie finished breakfast and began collecting a strange group of items. Half an hour later she went over her list of props, packing them into a shopping bag. "Scarves, fake daisies, old baseball cap, playing cards, teddy bear . . ." She sighed. She knew it wasn't enough. She still needed something guaranteed to bring screams of laughter. What would five-year-olds react to? The answer came in a flash: something messy. She giggled. What could be messier than a raw egg landing on her head? She bit her lip thoughtfully, visualizing the egg trickling down her face. Her mother kept a plastic rain bonnet in the hall closet; that would keep the egg off her green wig. The more she thought about her idea, the better she liked it.

The next step was the costume. Bobbie knew she could dress at Ellen's, but she wanted to take the time to make Bubbles perfect. She slipped into the baggy overalls and shoes, settled the wig over her own brown hair, and sat down in front of the mirror to apply the greasepaint. The white makeup felt slippery on her hand and surprisingly cool when she applied it. She covered every inch of her face with the white base. Next, she dabbed round brown spots across her nose and painted on wide black eyebrows and a huge, smiling mouth. She stood back to look at herself in the mirror, tilting her head from side to side.

"Not bad for a beginner," she said, pleased with her image.

Bobbie didn't have long to admire herself. There was a scrunching sound, and she looked out the window to see Ellen's car pulling into the driveway.

"Well, Bubbles," she said to her reflection, "your moment has come." Then she gathered up her things and went to meet her sister.

By the time Bobbie reached the car, Ellen had collapsed over the steering wheel, shaking with laughter.

"I don't believe it." She shook her head. "Bobbie, you look terrific. Amy is going to love you."

"She ought to," Bobbie said. "I'm her aunt. I just hope she loves Bubbles. Don't tell her it's me, OK?"

"Your secret's safe," Ellen promised, "but despite the super makeup job, I think she's going to recognize you. Those freckles are great, and so's the mouth."

Bobbie nodded. "I hate sad, droopy-mouthed clowns. I decided to make Bubbles look happy for her one-and-only public appearance."

When they pulled into Ellen's driveway, the butterflies fluttered in Bobbie's stomach. She felt a pang of regret. Maybe it was a mistake to go to the party as Bubbles. What if she bombed, and Amy and her friends hated her as a clown? Being rejected by a group of five-year-olds would be terrible. The thought made her slouch back against the seat. Her eyes mirrored the gloom while her big red lips smiled.

Ellen nodded toward the side door. "Come on, Bubbles. It's almost time for your debut. I asked Steve to have the camera ready to capture your entrance."

Steve Wilson's six-foot frame filled the doorway. As Bobbie eased herself out of the car, he aimed his camera. Bobbie struck a pose, lifting up one great shoe and nearly landing in the snow.

"Good," Steve said, "now lift the other one." Under her makeup Bobbie grinned. Steve was a tease, but he was also a super brother-in-law, with a build like a football player and a good head for real estate.

"Not bad," he told her, stepping aside as she and Ellen entered the house. "I sent Amy next door until party time so you can keep out of sight and surprise her."

He looked at Bobbie more closely. "I don't think she's going to recognize you."

"Aren't you going to stay to find out?" Bobbie asked. Steve was taking a long wool coat from the closet.

"Can't. I hate to snap and run, but I have an appointment in fifteen minutes to meet a client and show a house. Have fun." He pulled on his coat and bent to give Ellen a kiss. He grinned at Bobbie. "Sorry. I don't kiss clowns."

"See you later," Ellen told him, giving him a playful push out the door. "Now go, or you'll be late."

Bobbie peeked into the living room of the cozy ranch house. Bright red-and-white balloons and crepe-paper streamers hung from the ceilings. "It looks great," she told her sister. "You and Steve did a good job of decorating. Now, where do I put my bag of tricks?"

"Why don't you—" Ellen broke off as Amy's voice called, "Let us in, Mommy. It's cold out here."

"The bedroom," Ellen said and went to let her daughter in.

It wasn't long before Bobbie heard the chatter of several little girls and Ellen explaining that there was a surprise visitor. Quickly Bobbie stuffed her baggy pockets with the deck of playing cards and the silk scarves she had brought from home. At the moment she wasn't quite sure what she would do with them. She had a few ideas, but mainly she would play it by ear. Ellen knocked on the bedroom door. It was time for Bubbles to make her appearance.

When Bobbie shuffled into the living room, stumbling over imaginary obstacles on the floor, ten children, dressed in their party best, shrieked with laughter. At first Bobbie felt a little silly, but after one look at Amy's delighted face, she let the clown take over. Bobbie did some simple card tricks and then tried tying knots in handkerchiefs, but the knots kept coming untied. Next, she tried fancy dance steps which ended in clumsy falls, and finally, tying a rain scarf over her head, she held up an egg.

"This is a special trick," Bobbie told the ten wide-eyed girls as she broke the egg into an old, red baseball cap. "I'm going to turn this gooey egg into a chicken. If you watch very carefully he'll pop out of the cap." She waved a white-gloved hand over the tattered cap, mumbling, "Egg become a chicken, cluck, cluck, cluck . . ." Amy and her friends moved closer for a better view of the promised chicken. Bobbie glanced at Ellen, shrugged her shoulders, and continued her chant. She rolled her eyes and slapped the cap on top of her head. "Chicken, chicken, now appear . . . pleeeze," she moaned, removing the cap. Egg yolk dripped down onto her forehead and trickled down her white, freckle-painted face. Ten pairs of hands clapped wildly.

"Oh dear, oh dear," Bubbles exclaimed sadly. "This will never do. What happened to the chicken? Maybe he's in the other room!" She waved to her audience as she attempted her exit. The big shoes overlapped, and Bubbles stumbled and fell to her knees. She scrambled to her feet, stumbling again as she left the room. Shrill squeals of laughter and loud clapping made Bobbie's smile widen under the red curving lips.

"Come back, clown," Amy shouted.

"Come back!" all of Amy's friends cried.

Ellen came to the rescue. "Let's play a game while Bubbles washes the egg off her face. I'm sure she'll be back."

Bobbie went straight into the bathroom to remove the rain bonnet and wipe off the sticky yolk before repairing her makeup. The sound of laughter still echoed in her ears, and she could picture the excited looks on the kids' faces. They liked Bubbles, and she was glad.

The front doorbell rang, as she added more lipstick to the wide smiling mouth. It was probably the banjo player, she thought, re-touching her freckles. Quickly she surveyed her image in the mirror and, satisfied, went out to rejoin the party.

Bobbie followed the music into the living room, where a tall, sandy-haired boy who looked about seventeen stood strumming a banjo to a song about a fox. So this was Jay Hartwell, she thought, as she watched his fingers move deftly across the strings. Amy and her friends sat spellbound. *Guess they think he's good-looking, too,* Bobbie thought to herself.

Jay finished the song and smiled at his young audience. "Now I want you to sing," he told them. "You all know 'Old MacDonald.' " He strummed a few chords.

Bobbie's grin widened. Did she dare join his act? This was her chance.

In the middle of "Eeee-yi, oh," Bubbles stumbled into the room to lend her voice. Amy and two others ran over to her at once, laughing, but still singing at the top of their lungs. This broke up the chorus a bit. Luckily, Jay didn't seem to mind being upstaged. When the song ended, he put down his banjo and shook his head. "That's the most enthusiastic 'Old MacDonald' I've ever heard. You sure you didn't coach them?" he said to Bobbie.

"She did not," Ellen replied with mock indignation. "That was this clown's first song. Jay, meet my sister, Bobbie Reese, also known as Bubbles the Clown."

Bobbie shook Jay's extended hand. "Hi, Jay," she said. "I like your music. You're really good on that banjo."

"Thanks." He gave her an infectious smile. "You make a terrific clown."

Bobbie let her eyes roll comically. "I hope so. This is my big debut, and I don't want bad reviews."

Ellen had called the kids into a circle for a game, and Bobbie shuffled to the end of the room to get out of the way. Jay followed. For a few minutes they watched quietly as Ellen and her neighbor, Suzanne Wright, tried to organize a simple game where the children dropped clothespins into a jar. About half the guests were willing to go along with this; the rest wanted to throw the clothespins at one another. Bobbie knew she should help, but her long shoes seemed glued to the spot near

Jay. He looked straight at her as if trying to see the real person behind the makeup and the baggy costume. Fortunately, the white greasepaint kept him from seeing the blush she knew covered her face.

"We should help. . . ." she murmured.

His grin warmed her to her toes. "Why don't we take over the next game?"

Bobbie nodded. "Good idea."

Jay put his banjo in its case and took her hand, pulling her toward the noisy group of five-year-olds.

Ellen had given up on the clothespin idea. She now stood in the middle of the room, waving a piece of paper. "Next we'll play Pin the Tail on the Donkey," she said, pointing to a large, tailless paper donkey on the wall.

"We'll take over for you, if you want," Bobbie told her sister.

Jay laughed. "I might even play. It's been a long time since I've pinned the tail."

"I never found the donkey," Bobbie admitted. "I always ended up pinning the tail on the nearest person."

"Remind me to stay out of your way," Jay said.

Grateful for a chance to relax, Ellen and Suzanne Wright sat down and let Bobbie and Jay take over. The noise in the room grew louder as Bobbie blindfolded each girl in turn and Jay gave everyone a paper tail with a strip of tape at the end. Squeals of laughter filled the room as each girl tried to find her way to the donkey.

"You still want to play?" Bobbie asked.

Jay grinned and knelt to spin Peggy Wright back toward the donkey. "No way," he said. "I forgot how hard it was."

When the game ended at last, Amy and her friends surrounded Bobbie and Jay, eager to talk to them and touch Bubbles's fuzzy wig.

Chapter Two

The children called for more and more of Bubbles's antics and more songs from Jay. Though the baggy costume was hot and the greasepaint felt sticky, Bobbie ignored the discomfort.

Finally Ellen served the birthday cake, and Bobbie went into the kitchen for a break. She had just opened a can of soda and sat down at the table, when Jay walked in. Without a word, he sat down directly across from her, studying her face with curiosity.

Bobbie tilted her head to one side, then the other. "Are my freckles on crooked?" she asked, crossing her eyes as she tried to see the end of her nose.

Jay laughed. "I'm trying to see the real you.

It isn't easy, you know. Are you really scowling under that red grin?"

She sipped her soda, her heart thumping faster. Was he really interested in her, she wondered, or was he just making conversation? " 'Keep them guessing' is my motto," she told him, and then wondered frantically if she had said the wrong thing.

Jay's eyes lit up when he smiled. "Fair enough, Bobbie 'Bubbles' Reese. Look, when the party starts up again, do you want to help me teach the kids a round? They usually go wild over 'Row, Row, Row Your Boat.' How about it? Will you help me out?" He looked straight into Bobbie's eyes.

Bobbie nodded. "Sure. Why not?" Actually, it sounded like fun. Jay was fun. In fact, he was terrific. She was beginning to think that putting on the clown outfit was the smartest thing she had done in ages. If she hadn't, she never would have met Jay. She hated to think of the party ending.

The rest of the afternoon went by swiftly. Before she knew it, parents began arriving to pick up their children.

"I don't want to go," one little girl with pigtails exclaimed when her mother insisted she put on her coat.

"Can't we stay longer?" another wanted to know.

In spite of the protests, soon only Amy and Ellen, Peggy and Suzanne Wright, and Jay and Bobbie remained. Suzanne Wright slipped into her coat before joining Bobbie and Jay in the living room, where they sat drinking leftover fruit punch.

"You two were terrific," she told them. "You have a special way with children. I'd like to hire you to perform at my son Tommy's birthday party next weekend. He's going to be seven, and I know he and his friends would love you. Please say you'll do it."

Bobbie sighed, shaking her green-topped head. "I'm sorry, Mrs. Wright. This was just a special one-time appearance for Amy. Bubbles is retiring as soon as I get home."

Peggy pulled her red stocking cap over her head. "Come to the party," she begged, tugging on Bobbie's sleeve. "Maybe I can see you again. I can be there, can't I, Mom? Please?"

"Bobbie said she can't make it," Mrs. Wright told her daughter quietly.

Ellen was busy taking down the crepe-paper streamers. "I think you two should do it," she said. "You proved today that you have a special gift. You saw how the kids loved you. One more party won't take much of your time, and it would make a little boy happy."

"Me, too," Peggy cried, clapping her hands.

Bobbie hesitated for a moment, then shook

her head. "I can't. I'm sorry. I belong to the math club at school, and it keeps me busy most Saturdays, either with meetings or studying for monthly competitions."

Jay shrugged. "That's too bad." He turned to Mrs. Wright. "If you'll settle for a folk singer, I'm available."

"Fine," Suzanne Wright agreed. "I'll phone you with details tomorrow. I'm just sorry Bobbie can't come, too. I know Peggy is going to be talking about you both for days."

"Bye, Bubbles," Peggy called over her shoulder as her mother steered her out the door.

Bobbie waved to the little girl. "Bye, Peggy. I'm glad you had fun."

When the door closed behind them, Jay stood up, stretching. "This has been quite a day, and I have to get home for dinner." He picked up his banjo and headed toward the hall closet for his jacket.

Bobbie jumped to her feet, stumbling over the floppy clown shoes. If Jay left then she would never see him again. The warmth she had felt drained away. She looked at Ellen, desperately hoping her sister could read her mind.

Ellen stuffed the last crepe-paper streamer into a plastic bag and came to the rescue. "Could you drop Bobbie off on your way? It would save me the drive, if it's not too much out of your way. I want to finish cleaning here."

Jay glanced at Bobbie, grinning. "Sure. I was about to suggest it, but I thought she might be staying with you. How about it, Bobbie. Would you like a lift?"

"I'd love it," Bobbie said. She gave Ellen a hasty glance. "If you're sure I can't help you."

"I can help Mommy," Amy said firmly. "I can put the paper plates and cups in the trash bags, can't I, Mommy? Please?"

Ellen laughed. "See, you don't have to worry about me. I've got plenty of help. Besides, you've already been a lifesaver today by making the party a big success."

A cold wind was blowing when Bobbie and Jay stepped outside. Fine snow made little swirls on the hood of Jay's car, a 1971 Ford that looked as though it had seen better days. The motor started with an effort, groaning before it finally turned over.

"The heater in this heap isn't the greatest," Jay said apologetically.

Bobbie shrugged. "I'm fine." Actually, she was very cold, but she didn't care about the temperature. She was just glad to be with Jay in his battered old car.

And even though she wasn't crazy about country music, she didn't mind when he flipped on the radio and searched for a country station.

"So, do you like this kind of music?" he asked.

She shrugged. "I like some of the crossover singers like Dolly Parton and Kenny Rogers."

A mellow-sounding guitar solo followed the vocal, and Bobbie smiled as she watched Jay's fingers tap the rhythm on the steering wheel.

The song ended as they pulled into the Reese driveway. "That Chet Atkins sure can play," he said, reaching across to open the door.

Bobbie nodded, wanting desperately to keep the conversation going and not having the faintest idea of what to say. "Thanks for the ride" was what she came up with. "You know," she went on, suddenly nervous, "I didn't want to dress up in this clown suit today, but now I'm glad I did. It was fun." *Better stop now before you say something silly*, she told herself. She eased herself out of the car. This was it. The end of a perfect day.

Jay leaned over. "I had a good time, too," he said. "You take it easy now." Then he backed the car out of the driveway and drove off.

Bobbie watched until he turned the corner before going into the house. A sudden letdown feeling swept over her. Jay was special.

He was warm and friendly, not to mention talented. And he made her feel as if they had been friends for a long time. Would she ever see him again, she wondered.

By the time she went upstairs, scrubbed off the thick greasepaint, changed into her favorite jeans and a sweatshirt, and hurried down to the kitchen, it was already time for supper. Bobbie automatically started the meal. Whenever she could Bobbie took over cooking some of the meals. Usually, she didn't mind. In fact, she enjoyed cooking, being creative and trying new recipes.

As soon as she peeled the potatoes and slid a pan of breaded pork chops into the oven, she sat down at the table, picked up the phone, and dialed Nancy's number.

Nancy answered the phone in a ridiculously prim voice. "Good evening. Miz Stewart speaking. May I help you?"

"You're lucky it's only me on the phone, Miz Stewart," Bobbie said with a laugh. "What a phony! I'm glad you're home, though. I called to fill you in on my afternoon. It turned out to be fantastic!"

"What happened? I thought you were going to help Ellen with Amy's party. That was fantastic?"

Bobbie smiled smugly into the phone. "It sure was, and Bubbles was a great success."

25

"Who or what is Bubbles?" Nancy wanted to know.

"I went as a green-haired, freckle-faced clown," Bobbie told her friend. "The kids loved me. And, Ellen hired a gorgeous banjo player. His name's Jay Hartwell, and he goes to East High. I couldn't believe how nice he was."

Nancy moaned. "I can't let you out of my sight for a minute, can I?"

"Do I detect a slight hint of envy?" Bobbie teased. "Actually, I didn't want to go as a clown. It was Ellen's brainstorm, but now I'm glad I did."

"I'm sure you were thrilling," Nancy said impatiently, "but tell me more about this Jay person. Is he going to call you?"

"Nancy," Bobbie moaned, "we just met. We didn't make any plans. Actually, my sister's friend asked us to entertain at her son's birthday party, but I don't think I can. There's another math competition coming up, and I should do some studying."

"Get someone to fill in for you," Nancy advised. "I bet George wouldn't mind."

"Probably not." It was true. George Willis had been Bobbie's friend since kindergarten. Because he wasn't very athletic and wore thick, dark-rimmed glasses, a lot of the kids at school called him a nerd. But to Bobbie, he was a brilliant math student and a nice guy. Like Bobbie, he loved the challenge of solving abstract problems. But what was most important to Bobbie was that he was her good friend, someone she could really count on.

Bobbie glanced at the clock above the refrigerator. "I have to get supper on now," she told Nancy. "I'll call you tomorrow. OK?"

They hung up just as Mr. and Mrs. Reese walked through the back door.

"How was Bubbles?" asked Mr. Reese. "Was it as bad as you thought it'd be?"

Mrs. Reese looked at her daughter, smiling. "It was sweet of you to do it, hon. I know you really didn't want to. Maybe I should have thrown out that costume after all."

"That's OK, Mom." Bobbie took out the silverware and began setting the table. "It wasn't so bad."

"Not so bad?" Mr. Reese demanded indignantly. "You shorten the costume I have loved for twelve years, wear it to my granddaughter's birthday party, and all you can say is, 'It wasn't so bad'?"

Bobbie couldn't hide the grin any longer. "All right, Dad. If you want the truth, it was great!"

That night Bobbie filled two pages in her diary with descriptions of the party, her clown act, and Jay Hartwell. The last thing she heard before drifting off to sleep was the grandfather clock striking ten—and she could have sworn she heard faint banjo music in the background.

The sound of sleet hitting the windows woke Bobbie the next morning. It was Sunday, a day for sleeping late and lounging around the house, doing nothing in particular. So it was a while before she persuaded herself to get out of bed.

She had just put some opalescent polish on her nails when her mother called up the stairs, "Telephone for you, Bobbie. It's a boy, but it doesn't sound like George."

Bobbie's heart was pounding when she picked up the phone. "Hi," she said.

"Hi, yourself," a cheerful voice replied. "How's my favorite clown today?"

"Jay?" She couldn't believe it.

"I looked your number up in the phone book. I hope you don't mind my calling." He sounded apologetic.

Bobbie's heart thumped harder. Mind? It was terrific! "It's good to hear from you."

"I've been thinking about Mrs. Wright's invitation," he told her. "We were a good team, Bobbie. Why don't we do the act one more time?"

"I've been thinking about it, too," she ad-

28

mitted. "I'll skip math club this week. It won't hurt this once."

"I knew it," he said, his voice teasing.

"Knew what?"

"Knew that you were stagestruck the minute you stumbled into my 'Old MacDonald.' Better face it, Bobbie. Bubbles has a hold on you."

"Maybe," Bobbie said. It was easier than admitting that *he* had a hold on her. "I'm not so sure about being stagestruck, but I'll give it one more try."

"Good. I'll pick you up and take you to the party. And I'll call you tomorrow night."

Minutes after they'd hung up, Bobbie was still holding the phone, staring at it. The memory of Jay's voice and the alive, happy feeling she had when she played the clown were still with her. She had just one wish, and she whispered it to herself, "I hope this week goes quickly."

Chapter Three

On the Monday after Amy's party, Bobbie found herself the center of attention as her friends clustered around their lockers. Nancy stood by looking innocent as the others fired questions at Bobbie.

"I hear you're wearing greasepaint these days," Tom Hopkins said, tossing his books onto a top shelf and pulling out a notebook.

"Yeah, and I wonder where you heard it," Bobbie said, glaring at her best friend.

"*Why* would you want to play a clown?" Gloria Storrell asked. She was peering into a mirror on the inside of her locker door and combing her bangs.

Bobbie shrugged. "Kids like clowns."

"I can't picture you wearing a clown suit,"

George told her. "I hope your sister took some pictures. I want to see this."

"I'm sure you do," Bobbie snapped. Even George was irritating her that day. She pulled her English and math books from her locker and slammed the door. "And, I might do it again." She turned and walked toward her homeroom.

Nancy hurried to catch up to her. "I'm sorry. You don't really mind that I told them, do you?"

Bobbie shook her head. "Not if they don't make a big deal of it." She stopped and looked at her friend. "It's just that I really liked it, and they turn everything into a joke—Nancy, I'm going to do that other party."

"With Jay?"

"He called me yesterday. We're going to—"

The first bell rang, and they broke off, hurrying toward their homerooms. The image of Bubbles's painted face filled Bobbie's mind She'd have to come up with something new for the green-haired clown.

When Saturday rolled around, Bobbie dressed in her Bubbles outfit, applied her greasepaint, and then waited for Jay to pick her up. A thousand butterflies danced in her stomach. It wasn't the thought of playing the clown that made her nervous; it was the thought of seeing Jay again. She wanted him to like her, but how could he get to know Bobbie Reese if he only saw her bundled in the clown outfit, her face hidden under tons of white makeup? Would he like her if he saw the real Bobbie? It was strange, but the makeup made her feel more secure.

Unable to calm down, she went into the kitchen, where her parents were eating lunch. Her father had had the time to come home that day.

Her mother looked up and shook her head in disbelief. "You've got to let me take a picture of this!"

Bobbie rolled her eyes and then obligingly posed, perched crazily on one big foot, her arms waving in the air. "My daughter the clown," Mrs. Reese murmured.

"Absolutely terrific," her father pronounced. "But you might want to dust some talcum powder over that white makeup."

"What for?" Bobbie asked, wishing she had remembered to eat *before* painting on the red mouth.

"It's an old trick I learned years ago. The powder soaks up some of the grease. You put it on very heavily and brush the excess off."

It sounded like a good idea. "Thanks, Dad. I'll give it a try."

After quickly eating her lunch, Bobbie went

up to her room and found that her father's trick worked. She was making a final adjustment to the wig when she heard Jay's car swing into the drive.

"Stop being nervous," she told her reflection sternly. "After all, it's just a bunch of seven-year-olds." But it wasn't the thought of the party that made her heart turn over. It was Jay Hartwell.

Bobbie pulled her winter jacket over the clown suit and went out to the car. She pulled open the door and slid in beside Jay.

"Morning, Miss Bubbles," he said, backing out of the driveway. "Did I tell you? We're going to be paid the princely sum of twenty-three dollars. That's eleven-fifty apiece."

"Oh," Bobbie said. She hadn't even thought about money.

"Which means," Jay went on, "that you are now a professional. Ready to break a leg?"

"No way," Bobbie answered. "I know that's what they say in show business, but I broke my ankle when I was ten, and eight weeks in a cast was enough for a lifetime."

For the first time that morning, she let herself really look at Jay. His thick, sandy hair fell to just above the collar of his down jacket, and his eyes were a dark, almost indigo blue. He was even better looking than she had remembered.

"You know," he teased, "it isn't every guy who gets to ride around with a girl with green hair."

Suddenly Bobbie wished she weren't in her ridiculous getup. There she was, sitting next to the cutest guy she had ever met, and she looked like a refugee from a Saturday-morning cartoon.

"And," he went on more seriously, "it isn't often I meet someone who's so good at making kids laugh."

"I had a lot of fun last week," she said.

"So did I." Jay was smiling at her now, and her doubts about the clown suit vanished. "Hey, you nervous?" he asked.

"A little," she admitted.

"Well, don't be," he said gently. "It'll be just like last week. We'll leave 'em wanting more."

And they did. In fact, Tommy's party was even more successful than Amy's. Bobbie had a few more tricks up her baggy sleeves, and Jay had an endless repertoire of folk songs.

Bobbie even came up with some spur-of-the-moment props in Mrs. Wright's kitchen. And since the egg trick had been such a success, she decided to repeat it with a light variation. This time, she ceremoniously spread a newspaper on the floor.

35

"I'll need your help with this one, banjo player," she said to Jay.

The moment she held up a large egg, Peggy Wright squealed. "Make it into a chicken this time, Bubbles."

"Don't be dumb, Peggy. She can't do that," Tommy Wright said.

Bobbie chuckled. "I'm not going to try. This is a new trick, Peggy." She placed the egg in a pan and gently stirred it with a wooden spoon. "Egg, egg, become hard boiled," she chanted, then scooped it onto the spoon and tossed it to Jay. The egg broke in his hands, and he tried desperately to keep it from trickling onto the paper at his feet. Instead, the egg slithered up his arm. Jay shot Bobbie a disbelieving look and moaned loudly. She rushed to his rescue, wiping the mess with one of her bright kerchiefs. Then she turned slowly toward the door, head bowed. "I'm a failure," she sobbed through her mock tears, "a terrible, dismal failure."

The boys laughed, but Peggy rushed to Bubbles's side, hugging the baggy costume. "No you're not, Bubbles. I love you."

Jay quietly left to wash the egg off his hands, then returned and picked up the banjo. His nimble fingers picked out a popular song, and Tommy and his friends began to sing.

Later, while the children noisily gobbled

chocolate cake and fudge-ripple ice cream, Mrs. Wright joined Bobbie and Jay in the living room. "This is for you," she said, handing them each an envelope. "You really earned it."

"That was an interesting little change you made in the egg trick," Jay said as they rode home.

Bobbie looked at him doubtfully. "Did you mind?"

"You could have given me a little warning," he said, laughing.

"I didn't have time," she told him. "It was one of those moments of pure inspiration."

"Well, next time you get one of those inspirations, give your partner time to prepare himself."

Partner? Bobbie wondered if she had heard him right.

Jay pulled up in front of her house. "How about going out for pizza to celebrate another brilliant—excuse me, *inspired*— performance?"

"I'll think about it," Bobbie teased.

"Good. I'll pick you up in an hour."

Bobbie watched until Jay's car was out of sight before going inside to the warmth of the hallway. For a moment she stood staring at the grandfather clock. In less than an hour

Jay would return and see her for the first time without her clown makeup. What would he think of her, she wondered? What should she wear? With a low moan she headed up the stairs and straight to the blue-and-white tiled bathroom.

It took a while to scrub away the greasepaint, shower, and search for just the right clothes to wear. She searched through the cedar closet in her room. For this date she wanted to look special. Her new jeans would be fine, but picking a top wasn't easy. She rejected about a dozen blouses before settling on her pink cotton sweater. It would be perfect. She rarely wore makeup, but for this occasion she applied a touch of pale lipstick and a hint of eye shadow above her deep brown eyes. Her long dark hair looked best hanging loose, she decided, brushing it to a shine and letting it cascade over her shoulders. Finally, she stood back to stare critically at her image in the mirror. Would Jay approve? Suddenly she felt very nervous about their next meeting.

The front doorbell rang, and Bobbie heard her parents' voices. She paused a moment at the head of the stairs to listen; Jay was introducing himself. Then she took a deep breath and quickly made her entrance.

Jay's eyes widened when he saw her. "So

this is the face behind the clown," he said. "You look terrific."

Relief surged through her. "Thanks. I see you've met my parents already."

He nodded, taking her coat from her and helping her into it. Maybe he was trying to make points, she thought, but she liked the treatment anyway.

The Pizza Palace was crowded, as usual. Bobbie and Jay found a table in the corner, and Jay ordered "one with everything."

"Except anchovies," Bobbie told him, wrinkling her nose. "I can't stand those salty little fish."

"Right. Keep the little salty fish in the fishbowl," he told the waitress.

"So, while we're waiting for our pizza, how about filling me in on Bobbie Reese?" Jay said.

Bobbie felt her color rise. "There isn't much to tell. I'm a sophomore at Wilson High, and I really like math. You met my parents, my sister, and Amy. I also have a big brother in the navy and a brother-in-law who's a great guy. Right now, my big brother's on a submarine in the Mediterranean." She gave him a smile. "That's about it. Roberta Reese in a small nutshell."

Jay shook his head. "There has to be a lot

39

more, but that's OK. I'll find out the rest next time."

His words sent her blood racing. There was going to be a next time.

"I have some news," he said. "Just before I picked you up, I got a phone call from Dr. Jameson, an administrator at Langston Hospital. He wanted to know if I could play the banjo at a party on the pediatric ward next Saturday afternoon. I played there a couple of times before Christmas. I told him about our act, and he wants you, too. It doesn't pay anything, but it's for a good cause."

Bobbie stared at the checked tablecloth. Should she say yes and play the clown one more time? She bit her lip, remembering the big math competition slated for Saturday at the Convention Center in the city. The suburban Wilson team had a good chance of winning against the top city school. It was one of the biggest contests of the year. Why did there always have to be choices? She wanted to do both. "What did you tell Dr. Jameson?" she asked.

Jay smiled. "I told him I'd have to ask you, but that I thought we'd both be there. No kidding, those kids really love it when performers come to the hospital. I'll bet they'd fall in love with Bubbles; they might even forget that they're sick for a while. How about it? Will you do the act with me?"

Bobbie shrugged. A vision of children in wheelchairs and hospital beds flashed through her mind. It could be depressing. On the other hand, if she and Jay could cheer them up, even for a little while, it would be worth doing the act.

"All right," she said. "I'll do it. My math teacher's not going to be too happy when I tell her I'm not going to be in the competition, but . . ."

The waitress set their pizza in front of them. Jay waited until she left before reaching across the table to squeeze Bobbie's hand. "I knew I could count on you," he said. "You're the greatest."

The greatest what, she wondered. *Traitor to my math club? Pushover for indigo-blue eyes?* She took a bite of her pizza, savoring the spicy tomato sauce. Had she done the right thing? It seemed crazy to feel so guilty about skipping a math competition.

Jay looked puzzled. "There's no problem, is there?" he asked. "I guarantee, when you do a show for those kids in the hospital, you're going to want to do more. You'll see."

"I hope so," Bobbie said quietly. After skipping that afternoon's meeting, she dreaded facing Miss Jordan, her math teacher.

41

On Monday morning Bobbie left study hall early to speak to Miss Jordan before math class.

The teacher looked up from the test she was correcting. "Hello, Bobbie," she said. "You're awfully early."

Bobbie shifted her books from one arm to the other. "I'd like to talk to you, if you have a minute."

Miss Jordan glanced at her watch. "We have a few minutes before class. What can I help you with? You're not worried about the competition, are you?"

"No, but I want to talk to you about it. I . . ." She took a deep breath before going on. "I won't be able to be there, Miss Jordan. You see, I've been doing a clown act for parties, and this Saturday there is a very special one in the children's ward at the hospital."

Miss Jordan's voice was quiet. "And is this party more important than the competition?"

"Not exactly," Bobbie admitted, "but the kids are sick, and the show my friend and I do may make them forget their problems for a while. I think that's important, too. That's why I said I'd do the show."

The teacher stared thoughtfully at Bobbie, then nodded. "I can see that this wasn't an easy choice for you. Don't worry. I'll assign someone else to take over for you Saturday. You go ahead and entertain those kids."

Bobbie was staring at her open locker, trying to figure out which books to take home, when George, Nancy, and Bill Daniels came up to her.

"Miss Jordan told us you wouldn't be at the Convention Center Saturday," George said.

Nancy looked at her with concern. "That's not like you. What gives?"

Bobbie shrugged. "I'm going to entertain at a party in the children's ward at Langston Hospital on Saturday. I wish I could be in two places at the same time, but I can't."

"I thought you liked being on the math team," George said.

"I do," Bobbie assured him. "But when I see kids laughing and having a good time when I dress up as a clown, I get a really special feeling. It's hard to explain."

Bill thumped George on the back. "Well, George will hold your spot for you—if he can leave his computer long enough, that is."

George said nothing but stared at Bobbie, his eyes unreadable behind the dark-rimmed glasses.

"I'm sorry if I'm creating a problem," Bobbie said, taking out her history and English books. "This is something I just have to do. No, that's not true. I just want to entertain the kids, that's all." She closed her locker, turned, and left her friends standing in the hall.

That evening at the dinner table Bobbie was quiet.

"You have something on your mind," Mrs. Reese said, pouring herself a cup of tea. "I can tell."

Bobbie smiled in spite of herself. Sometimes it seemed as though her mother could read her mind.

"A problem?" her father asked.

"Well, I guess I should tell you. I've told Miss Jordan I can't be in the competition Saturday. She seemed to understand." There. It was out.

Her parents exchanged brief glances.

"Bobbie," her mother began, "I can understand how you must enjoy entertaining the children, but are you sure you want to drop out of the competition?"

"I'm sure, Mom," Bobbie answered. "I've given it a lot of thought, and this hospital party is important to me—more important than math, I guess." She laughed. "I never thought I'd say anything like that."

"Not all that surprising," said Mr. Reese

with a chuckle. "Maybe it's something about that clown suit. You start to feel as if the clown were a part of you."

Bobbie looked at her father in surprise. Though she hadn't been able to put it into words, he'd described exactly what she had been feeling. "That's it," she said. "Bubbles is a part of me I never knew existed. And now I need to give her the chance to make those kids happy."

"As long as *you're* happy with your decision, Bobbie," her mother said. "That's what's important."

"I know I'm doing the right thing," she assured them.

Jay arrived early on the day of their hospital appearance. This time Bobbie brought along a nylon duffel bag containing her jeans, a sweater, a large jar of cold cream, and plenty of tissues. She and Jay would probably stop to eat after the party, and she didn't intend to go as Bubbles.

"You're looking good," Jay said, as she got into the car. "Do I detect a touch of pink in your cheeks?"

Bobbie had added red circles to her cheeks and more freckles across her nose. "I thought I'd look healthier this way," she told him brightly.

"Yeah," he agreed, "Bubbles always was a little pale, but I liked her anyway."

Bobbie didn't have an answer for that, so she leaned back and enjoyed the drive across town. They listened to Jay's tape deck, each lost in thought. Bobbie was going through a mental rehearsal of her act, and by the time Jay drove into the hospital parking lot, the feeling of anticipation made her stomach ache.

She was glad when Jay picked up his banjo in one hand and took her arm in the other. The slushy parking lot had a few water-filled potholes, and the big shoes made her stumble more than once. It was the kind of late January day that ate into a person's bones. It wasn't freezing, just damp.

Inside the hospital, they crossed the lobby to the elevators. Visitors, doctors, and orderlies all turned to stare. Bobbie waved to two small children seated beside an elderly man.

The elevator whisked them to the fourth floor pediatrics ward, where a nurse greeted them. Bobbie noticed the strong smell of antiseptic in the air.

"You must be Jay and Bubbles," the nurse said, smiling pleasantly. "The children are all out in the solarium having cookies and ice cream, waiting for you to arrive. I should warn you, Channel Five has sent a reporter, and she's waiting with cameras ready. You two will be instant celebrities by evening. Dr. Jameson thought it would be good publicity for the hospital. You know, a human-interest story."

Bobbie's stomach churned at the thought of cameras focused on her. Jay grinned. "Hey, that's terrific."

"I can't believe it!" Bobbie said, shaking her green head. "Me, Bobbie Reese, on television!" The thought stayed with her as they followed the nurse to the sun room, where the sound of children's voices greeted them.

Chapter Four

As Bobbie and Jay walked through the door-way of the solarium, the channel five camera-man focused his camera on them. In front of him, a group of kids clapped wildly. Bobbie froze. This was no living-room party. They were on TV. Jay gave her a little nudge.

Bobbie hadn't taken two steps into the room before her clumsy shoes overlapped, tripping her. She flung her arms to keep her balance, and a delighted audience broke into laugh-ter. Jay went along with what seemed to be part of their act. He stood by, shaking his head sadly at Bobbie. Seeing the reaction to her near-fall, Bobbie improvised. She clutched wildly at Jay, keeping her footing only to stum-ble again on the shoes. Finally, after several attempts, she regained her balance and waved at the camera, blowing a kiss toward the intimidating lens. The cameraman grinned as he zoomed in on Bobbie's face, and she gave him a toothy smile, completely caught up in the act of being a clown. The lens didn't seem as frightening now.

"Do that again," a small red-haired boy in a wheelchair called to her.

Bobbie noticed the bulky cast on the boy's leg. "I might fall and break my leg," she said, in her high Bubbles voice.

"Go ahead," a dark-eyed little girl shouted. "Stumble on your shoes."

Jay grinned at her and leaned close to whisper, "Your public calls. Let's see you repeat that entrance."

Bobbie deliberately let her shoes overlap as she walked to the front of the room, stumbling and almost going down. A boy of eleven or twelve jumped up to help her. "Thank you, sir," Bobbie said. Her voice faltered as she noticed an ugly burn scar on his cheek. Quickly, she gave him a big smile. "I don't understand it," she said to him. "My feet seem to have shrunk. My shoes don't fit anymore."

Jay took over then, making his way through rows of wheelchairs, urging the kids to sing along with him. When he played a sunny

Irish folk song, Bobbie joined him with the most uncoordinated jig she could manage. The audience loved it. Next, she and Jay went into their song routine, teaching the words to the kids and conducting a long, chaotic round. For her final act, Bobbie put on the rain bonnet and performed her egg trick. Giggles and howls of laughter echoed through the room. Even the cameraman was laughing.

As Bobbie took a bow before her cheering audience, she noticed a thin-faced little boy, hooked up to an intravenous tube, watching solemnly. *Why didn't I notice him before,* she wondered. She blew a special kiss his way and saw him smile.

Finally the show was over. Bobbie followed one of the nurse's aides to the women's lounge where she removed her makeup. Although she felt hot and sticky from having been under the lights, she found herself somehow reluctant to take off the costume. The day had been special, and she didn't want to let go of it.

Jay was waiting for her downstairs in the lobby. He took her hand. "We really did it this time. Did you hear those kids? They didn't want us to leave."

"I didn't want it to be over, either, though I wasn't too happy about the way I started.

You knew that my entrance was no joke, didn't you?"

Jay grinned. "I just figured you were being your normal, graceful self."

Bobbie felt her face turn red. "I was so embarrassed until I realized everyone thought it was part of the act. I was sure I was going to land on my seat. And you were no help."

"You didn't need my help," Jay said, as he pulled on his jacket. "You were doing just fine on your own."

They walked out to the car, arm in arm. Being with Jay seemed like the most natural thing in the world. It was hard to believe that just that morning she'd been so nervous about seeing him again.

"Where would you like to go?" Jay asked, as he opened the door with a gallant bow. "How about the Burger Barn?"

"And miss the evening news?"

"Oh, right," he said, sliding in next to her. "The weather report's supposed to be pretty exciting."

"You know," she told him, "I'm not the only clown around here."

Jay smiled at her. "Guilty." He let the engine idle for a moment. "What if we pick up some takeout Chinese and go back to your house to watch the news?"

"Sounds good."

"Bobbie—" His voice had gone suddenly husky. "I—I really like you. I feel good when we're together."

Bobbie felt a warm glow spread through her body. "I know. I mean, I feel the same way about being with you." She bit her lip. Why was it so hard to actually say these things? Jay was looking at her, his blue eyes serious. One day she'd have to get used to the fact that he was so good-looking. "Jay?"

"What?"

She told him the truth. "I've never been so happy."

Later that evening Bobbie's parents joined them in the living room for the news. After what seemed like an endless stream of reports on national events, the word *Special* flashed across the screen.

"Today," began the local announcer, "fun ruled on the children's ward at Langston Hospital, thanks to the combined talents of two local teenagers. Jay Hartwell's magic fingers made beautiful music on the strings of his banjo, and Bobbie Reese's vibrant personality brought laughter through her creation, Bubbles the Clown. Here are a few of the highlights, taped during their act."

Her father chuckled. "I believe you do that clown suit justice." He turned to her mother.

"You see? I always told you she took after me."

Mrs. Reese rolled her eyes. "Now don't start that again. . . ."

As her parents took up the familiar mock argument Bobbie felt Jay's hand secretly reach for hers, warm and reassuring. "What'd you think?" he asked.

Bobbie tried to keep a straight face. "You mean about the weather report?"

"Very funny. I mean about us."

Bobbie felt herself blush. "Even better than I thought," she told him.

The telephone on the end table rang. Mrs. Reese answered it, smiling. "Yes, Nancy, we saw the broadcast, and we're very proud of Bobbie." She held the phone out to her daughter. Reluctantly, Bobbie withdrew her hand from Jay's and got up to take the receiver.

"Hi, Nancy."

Nancy's voice was shrill with excitement. "Why didn't you tell me you were going to be on TV? Bill is here, and we just happened to see the news. Weren't you scared to face the camera? I would've been a wreck just thinking of all the people who were going to see me."

Bobbie laughed. "I was scared for a couple of minutes, but then I got involved in my act,

54

and I didn't have time to worry about the camera. How did you like our show?"

"Actually, you weren't bad. Bill and I sat here laughing at you. And Jay has a great voice. He's cute, too. No wonder you like him so much."

Bobbie glanced at Jay who was intently watching the day's sports highlights. "Who said I do?" she asked in a low voice.

"This is me, Nancy—your best friend, remember? I know you, Bobbie."

"We'll talk about it later," Bobbie told her. "Jay is here now, so I'd better go. I'll try to call you back tonight, OK?"

Bobbie put the phone down and curled up on the sofa beside Jay. Again his hand reached for hers. She glanced at him, shrugging. "That was my friend, Nancy. She saw us on the news and wanted to find out who the banjo player was. She thinks you have a great voice."

"Tell her I said thanks," he said. "Compliments never hurt."

Mrs. Reese started for the kitchen. "How does hot chocolate sound?"

Bobbie offered to help out, but Mrs. Reese shook her head. "You stay and talk with Jay and your father."

There was an awkward moment of silence, as the three of them wondered what they should be talking about. Finally, Mr. Reese leaned forward in his chair to face Jay. "So, how long have you been playing the banjo?"

"I took a few lessons when I was twelve," Jay told him, "and I've picked up a lot on my own, but I'd like to find a good instructor and go on with the lessons. Someday I'd like to play professionally—or maybe teach." He shrugged. "I'm not sure yet."

"Well, you certainly seem to have the talent," Mr. Reese said.

"Maybe." Jay's voice had become serious. "It's not easy to break into the music world. There's a lot of competition out there." He glanced at Bobbie. "That's why I'm glad to do these entertaining gigs. I need all the experience I can get."

"That's quite a practical approach."

Bobbie smiled. Her father seemed to like Jay, and that made her feel good.

Mrs. Reese returned with a tray of hot chocolate and oatmeal cookies. Bobbie had two more calls from school friends, anxious to tell her they'd seen her on the evening news. "Sorry about that," she apologized after the second call.

"Our daughter seems to be a celebrity," Mr. Reese told his wife.

Bobbie handed Jay a cup of steaming hot chocolate. "I think I've created a monster," she said. "I had no idea putting on that clown

suit for Amy was going to lead to all this."
She passed him the plate of cookies. "Try one
of these if you dare. Baked by the monster
herself."

"I'll take a chance," he said and promptly
downed three plump, raisin-filled oatmeal
cookies.

As soon as they had finished their refreshments, Jay got up to leave. "Thanks," he told
Mrs. Reese. Then he turned to Bobbie. "I'm
glad you let me invite myself over."

A half smile curved her mouth when she
looked up at him. "I'm glad you came."

Bobbie walked with Jay to the door. From
the living room windows, she watched him
walk down the drive. Then, with a sigh, she
went upstairs to her room. It was going to be
hard to bring herself back down to earth.

On Monday morning George met Bobbie at
her locker. "So," he said, smiling at her, "how
is our star today? I caught your act on TV.
You were actually quite good. I tried to phone
you, but your line was busy."

"That's probably because *I* was talking to
her," Nancy said, coming up behind them.
"Or maybe it was one of her other loyal fans.
You know how it is—the price of fame."

"Thanks," Bobbie said to George. Then to
Nancy she said, "Will you cut it out? It was a

busy day," she explained. "In fact, I didn't even hear how the math competition ended."

George shifted his books to the other arm. "Not good. We lost."

Bobbie quickly opened her locker and pulled out her books. "I'm sorry, George. I really am. I wish I could have been in two places at the same time."

Nancy tugged gently on her arm. "We'd better go, or we'll be late for homeroom."

"Right." Bobbie scrambled after her, dropping a notebook and hastily retrieving it. "See you," she called to George over her shoulder.

"Yeah, see you," he answered. "One of these days."

Tuesday afternoon was gray and cold. Nancy and Bobbie agreed that they might as well go to Bobbie's house and do homework; there was really nothing else to do. They were in the middle of conjugating French verbs when Jay phoned. "We have a chance to repeat our act," he said. "There's going to be a ward party at Strong Memorial Hospital this weekend."

Bobbie bit her lower lip.

"Did you hear me?" Jay asked.

"I heard you." She stared at the phone as if it could make her decision for her. "I'd like to do the act again, but I'm not sure if I should."

"Why not?"

"Math club meets Saturday," she told him. She covered the receiver and turned to Nancy. "What should I do?"

Nancy shrugged. "It's your problem, but I know what I'd do."

Bobbie sighed. "You mean quit math club?"

"It's the only solution to your problem, isn't it?"

Nancy was right, and Bobbie knew it. "I'll do the show, Jay," she said. "I'll just have to resign from math club. I can't keep asking for time off."

"You sure you want to do that?" he asked, surprised.

"Positive." And she was.

"That's great, Bobbie. You won't be sorry. I'll pick you up at two," he promised.

Bobbie hung up and turned to her friend. Nancy smiled. "Don't worry. The math team will survive, and you won't walk around looking so guilty."

"No kidding. I feel like seven pounds of lead have just been lifted from my back." She flopped down on the chintz-covered bed. "But, I sure hate making decisions."

"Welcome to the world," Nancy said with a decided lack of sympathy. She began to gather her books. "Now that we've solved your problem, I'd better get home." She glanced out the window. "It's starting to snow those big, heavy flakes. Maybe, if everyone in town stays up and prays all night, they'll close the schools tomorrow."

Bobbie joined Nancy at the window. Lazy white flakes fluttered to the ground. "Fat chance. Nothing short of an earthquake would make them close good old Wilson High."

The following morning the snow slowed travel, making almost everyone late for school. Bobbie had to wait until study hall before she had a chance to talk with Miss Jordan. She felt bad about having to tell the teacher that she was resigning from math club.

"You look like someone who still has a problem," the teacher said as Bobbie entered the room. "And I think I know what it is."

Bobbie's eyebrows arched in surprise. "You do?"

Miss Jordan put aside the lesson plan she'd been working on. "I've heard about your appearance at Langston Hospital, and I think it's wonderful. Unfortunately, you've discovered you're very human and can't do two things at the same time." Her eyes crinkled at the corners when she spoke. "Am I right? I rather expected it after our last meeting."

Bobbie heaved a sigh of relief. "I didn't think you'd understand the way I feel about entertaining. It gives me such a good feeling, Miss Jordan. When those sick little kids laugh, it's like music. But it's not going to be easy to give up the math club."

"You're wrong about my understanding, Bobbie. I do. And, you must do what you feel is best for you. We'll miss you in the math club, of course, but someone will take over your spot."

Nancy was waiting in the hall for her. "Don't move until you tell me what happened in there," she said, grabbing Bobbie's arm in a viselike grip.

"Nothing too dramatic," Bobbie assured her. "Miss Jordan was great, and I'm out of math club."

"I'm glad there was no problem," Nancy said. "Hey, look."

They watched a group of students working on the display case near the math room. They were tacking up a giant red heart-shaped poster proclaiming the annual Valentine's Day dance. Bobbie sighed. "It's strange the way some things change in seconds. A few weeks ago, if my friends had told me I'd drop out of math club, I would have said they were crazy."

Nancy pushed back her long blond hair. "As our French teacher would say, *C'est la vie.*"

Bobbie gave her a half smile. "Great. Here I am on the verge of a major guilt trip at dropping out, and you're giving me French clichés."

The bell rang, and Bobbie shifted her books. "We're going to be late for gym if we don't get going."

Nancy fell into step beside her. "The Valentine's Day dance will be here before we know it? Are you going to ask Jay?"

They turned the corner to hurry down a short hall. "I don't know." Actually, it hadn't even occurred to Bobbie. She knew Jay liked her, but they weren't exactly dating. "I—guess so," she said. She held up crossed fingers as they entered the gym. "I sure hope he says yes."

Chapter Five

On Saturday the sun shone brightly although there was a nip in the air. There were still patches of snow along the hedges and under the trees. Jay arrived right on time, and they listened to a banjo tape while they drove across town to the sprawling Strong Memorial Hospital.

It was just a matter of minutes until Bubbles made her stumbling entrance through the big doors of the sunroom. Her arrival brought instant laughter from the children, with one exception. Bobbie noticed a small, dark-eyed girl sitting off to the side in a wheelchair. Her thin, pale face was expressionless. Bobbie decided to play directly to the girl.

Her prop bag contained several items she

had never used. Bobbie pulled out a paper plate, a fork, and two slices of hard bread. She set them up on a hospital nightstand. "I'm so hungry," she moaned in her clown voice. "Do you mind if I have my lunch?"

Several little heads shook in reply. A chubby little girl called out, "I have a candy bar you can share."

Bobbie blew her a kiss. "That's nice of you, but this time I think I'll make a chicken sandwich."

"Where's the chicken?" asked a boy with a bandaged arm.

Bobbie rummaged in her shopping bag. "It's in here somewhere. I know it is. Chicken will taste so good." At last she pulled out a skinny rubber chicken, shaking her head. "I can't eat a rubber chicken," she said mournfully. Bobbie glanced at the little girl in the wheel-chair. Was that a hint of a smile on her face?

Later, after the clown act and sing-along had ended, Bobbie and Jay slipped out of the room to loud applause. A tall, graying doctor stopped them briefly in the hall. "You two deserve that applause," he told them, reaching out to shake their hands. "I watched part of the show, and you did a wonderful job." He looked at Bobbie, smiling. "Stick with it, young lady. The world needs more clowns.

Some of those kids in there haven't laughed since they were admitted."

He walked on then, but the words remained with Bobbie as she cleaned off her makeup and changed into her jeans and blue turtleneck sweater. On the drive home, she leaned her head back against the seat and closed her eyes.

"I can read your mind," Jay told her.

"I'll bet you can't."

"You're thinking about that little girl who doesn't laugh," he said.

Bobbie sat up. "How did you know?"

"I saw your reaction when she smiled at Bubbles. I think I heard one of the nurses call her Wendy."

"I wonder what's wrong with her. . . ."

"And," Jay went on, "you're probably wondering how old she is and how often her family comes to visit."

Bobbie looked at him in disbelief. "Am I that transparent?"

"It's not you," he said gently. "It's what's happening to you. Don't you see? You're hooked on making other people feel good. I knew it would happen."

"Did you? I didn't even know how I really felt. I thought I'd do the act a couple of times, and that would be it."

"That's how it starts, but the way you feel gets stronger each time you perform."

She nodded. "I still don't know how you were so sure I'd go on with Bubbles."

They had stopped at a light. Jay turned to look at her, and for a moment it seemed as if he could see straight into her heart. "Because it happened to me, too," he said quietly.

Later that night Jay phoned to tell her about a request for another performance. "The recreation director from Spring Lake Nursing Home asked if we could make an afternoon appearance this week. They wanted us for Valentine's Day, but I wasn't sure if you could make it that day."

"Well, my school's Valentine's Day dance is Friday, and Thursday the committees meet to decorate the gym and get everything set up. How about Wednesday after school?" Bobbie said, looking at her desk calendar. *I've got to ask him now,* she thought as Jay continued talking.

"Jay," she said hesitantly. "Now I have a question. I'm slow asking because I've been so busy I forgot about the dance, but—would you want to go with me?"

She heard him laugh. "Did you think I'd turn down my partner?"

She breathed a sigh of relief. "Terrific. You

can even come to the committee meeting, if you'd like, and help with the decorations. It'd be a good chance for you to meet my friends."

"Why not," he said. "We can talk about it Wednesday at the nursing home."

"Wait a minute," Bobbie said. "I just had an idea. Why don't I bake some cookies to take to the nursing home? I could make heart-shaped cookies and frost them red and white for Valentine's Day. I'll ask Nancy if she and Bill—that's her boyfriend—would like to help. It could be fun."

"I'll tell you what," Jay said. "I'll help you bake, too, as long as I can eat a few cookies while we work."

"Sounds fair to me," Bobbie agreed. "We'll make plenty for us and some for the nursing home, too."

Tuesday evening before the others arrived for the cookie baking, Bobbie and her mother made up several batches of dough and put them in the refrigerator to chill.

"You're on your own tonight," Mrs. Reese told Bobbie. "Your dad and I are going next door to the Potters' to watch a new video tape they bought. It's an old musical from the fifties." She did a couple of dance steps to illustrate.

Bobbie wrinkled her nose. "No offense, Mom, but I'd rather make cookies."

The doorbell rang, and Nancy and Bill came in, followed by Jay about ten minutes later.

Bobbie introduced everyone and led her crew to the kitchen. She took two batches of dough from the refrigerator. "Who wants to roll, and who wants to cut out?"

"I volunteer to frost and eat," Bill said.

"It figures," Nancy muttered.

Bobbie handed him the rolling pin. "For that, you get the first chance at the dough."

"You may want to reconsider," Nancy advised. "Last time I gave him a rolling pin, he absolutely murdered a perfectly innocent pie crust."

"It was anemic to begin with," Bill protested. And then, to prove himself, he floured an area of the counter and rolled out the dough with flawless technique.

"Allow me." Jay ceremoniously picked up the heart-shaped cookie cutter and quickly cut a dozen cookies.

"Admit it," Bill said, dabbing flour on Nancy's nose, "I'm a genius with a rolling pin." Nancy just shook her head and laughed.

As Jay slipped the cookies into the oven, Bobbie stared at Nancy's nose. "Maybe I could find a way to use flour in the act," she said.

"It would never work," Nancy told her. "How

would flour show up on Bubbles's face?" She picked up another ball of dough. "Who's next? Someone besides the genius here."

They had rolled out and cut two more sheets of cookies, when the oven timer buzzed, signaling that the first batch was ready. Bobbie removed the trays from the oven and used a spatula to scoop the cookies onto the waxed paper she had spread out on the counter. In seconds three hands reached out to snatch up the cookies, then drop them again.

"Man, they're hot," Bill exclaimed, shaking his hand.

"Yeah," Nancy agreed. "Things that have just been removed from the oven usually are."

The four spent the next two hours cutting, baking, frosting—and eating, ending up with a heaping tray of Valentine treats.

"Thanks, guys," Bobbie told Nancy and Bill when they finally put on their jackets to leave. "I appreciate your help."

Bill slipped his arm around Nancy's shoulders. "Hey, it was fun. No kidding."

Nancy nodded. "He always thinks eating's fun. See you in the morning, Bobbie."

With Nancy and Bill gone, the kitchen seemed suddenly quiet. Jay turned to Bobbie, putting his hands on her shoulders. "I enjoyed tonight. You've got nice friends," he said. "And this was a good idea." He gave her a quick kiss on the cheek, snatched a cookie from the platter, and disappeared through the doorway. "See you tomorrow night," he called over his shoulder.

Bobbie sighed deeply as she reached for the aluminum foil to cover the cookies. "See you, Jay," she answered.

On Wednesday afternoon, right after school, Jay picked Bobbie up, and they drove to the nursing home on the lakeshore. A few big snowflakes swirled in the air when they started out, but they turned into a full-scale squall by the time they reached their destination. Jay parked as near the rambling brick building as he could.

"This will pile up if it lasts more than ten minutes," Jay said as they got out of the car and hurried up the front walk. "Good thing I have decent snow tires."

Bobbie clutched her coat around her tightly. "I can't wait until spring." She felt nervous flutterings in her stomach when they entered the lobby. This was the first time she had been in a nursing home, and she wasn't sure of what to expect. The smell of antiseptic was almost overpowering when they walked down the corridor to the recreation room.

"What do we do with the cookies?" Bobbie whispered.

Jay motioned toward an open doorway near the room where they would entertain the patients. "I'll leave them with the recreation director. Want to come in with me?"

Bobbie shook her head. "I'll wait."

Jay disappeared into the office, and Bobbie leaned against the wall, thinking about how she would handle the act. Two elderly, white-haired women shuffled down the hall, smiling at her as they passed. She must look strange to them, she thought, with her green hair, clown makeup, and the baggy pants showing below her ski jacket. An old man parked his wheelchair directly in front of her. He gave her a hesitant smile. "Hello, there. You must be the young lady who's going to perform for us."

Bobbie smiled. "I hope so," she said.

"Then you just follow me," he said, executing a quick spin with the chair and heading for the recreation room.

Jay rejoined her in the doorway to the recreation room, where they waited until it was their time to entertain.

A plump, pleasant-faced woman was playing a lively polka on the piano, accompanied by a man with an accordian. Now and then, the assembled patients joined in on a line or two of a familiar song.

Bobbie leaned close to whisper in Jay's ear. "Let's do our original act."

"You mean 'Old MacDonald'?" He grinned at her. "Why not. They might get a laugh out of a kid's song. Let's do it."

The act went well. After a rousing round of folk songs, Bobbie's attempts at juggling two, then three and four beanbags brought smiles to the sternest faces. She danced to Jay's music, stumbled, and almost fell in the lap of a spry old man in the front row. Jay had a good sense for songs that the seniors would be familiar with; Bobbie could barely hear his voice above their enthusiastic singing. For the close of the act, she did card tricks, dropping the deck in a flurry of cards and ceremoniously bending to pick up first one card, then another. Finally, wiping her brow, she gave up and sat down to retrieve the rest. Amid laughter and clapping, Jay helped her up, and they took their bows. She and Jay went back to the hallway, while the patients enjoyed refreshments, including the colorful cookies they had brought.

Bobbie stood in the hallway, catching her breath and watching the patients, who were now being served beverages. She checked her watch. "The time went by so quickly."

"That's because they're such a great audience. I think we should do more shows in nursing homes. The recreation directors are always on the lookout for entertainers."

"Then let's do it again." She whirled around and almost lost her balance when the clumsy shoes overlapped. Jay reached out and caught her. "Thanks, partner," she said, righting herself. "That was no act. I just feel terrific!"

"I know." Jay's quiet voice told her he understood. Bobbie had had the same feeling at their other performances, but this was special. The happy looks on the faces of the elderly patients would remain with her always.

She changed into her jeans and sweater in the women's lounge and met Jay at the door. He was standing, banjo in hand, talking to a wrinkled, grizzly-faced old man in a wheelchair. "You must be Bubbles," said the man when he saw Bobbie. "You're a very special young lady. We need more like you." With those words he turned his chair around and took off down the hall.

Jay laughed. "What a guy. He's ninety, Bobbie. Ninety years old and still sharp." He reached out to brush a lock of hair from her face. "Do you want to go somewhere to eat?"

"I'd like to, but I'd better get home and do my homework. I didn't get much done with the baking last night."

He nodded. "I have to practice awhile."

The warm feeling stayed with Bobbie on

the drive back home. The snow had stopped, leaving the trees and rooftops wearing white coverlets. It looked like a fairyland, the perfect end to a wonderful day.

They said goodbye at the door, and Bobbie hurried inside, hanging her jacket in the hall closet before joining her parents in the living room.

"How did it go?" her mother asked.

Bobbie plopped down on the sofa. "I thought it might be boring at the home," she exclaimed. "Boy, was I wrong! Those people are a great audience. They liked us so much, we put on a longer show than usual without even realizing it."

Her father nodded. "It can get pretty lonely in a nursing home. Your show was probably a very special treat for them."

"I'm really glad we did it." Bobbie got up, started out of the room, then paused to look back. "The cookies were a big hit, too. Jay and I left when refreshments were being served, but I saw a lot of patients heading for the plate."

She hurried upstairs to settle herself at her maple desk with her English book, but she'd barely read two pages before the phone interrupted.

Nancy's voice was anxious. "I'm glad you're home. I just ran into George at the store, and

I thought I should warn you. He was all gloom and misery. He said Wilson lost the math competition by two points, and he's sure if you had been there we would have won."

Bobbie moaned. "Maybe and maybe not. I'm no guarantee of victory. Anyway, I'm out of it now. He'll just have to get used to it."

"How was the nursing home?" Nancy asked, quickly changing the subject.

"At first it was kind of depressing to see all those poor old people. But, you should have seen them laugh and heard them sing. It was as though they really loved us." She paused, tapping her pen against the desk. "And, as I told my mom, the Valentine cookies were a great success."

"Of course," Nancy said. "They were baked by four great cooks. Listen, try to think of some ideas to decorate the gym tomorrow. George is threatening to do something mathematical—two hearts adding up to one? I don't know."

Bobbie laughed. "I won't lose any sleep over it, but I'll see what I can come up with. I'd better get back to my homework, or I'll never finish. See you in the morning."

Chapter Six

"I think this looks ridiculous," George muttered as he perched on a ladder on one side of the gymnasium door.

"Just attach your wing and stop complaining," Bill ordered. They were hanging a very large and—to be fair to George—silly-looking Cupid over the doorway.

Nancy looked up from a riotous tangle of red-and-white crepe-paper streamers. "I think it looks great."

"You're only saying that because Bill would kill you if you didn't," George said, climbing down from the ladder. "Hey, who's that?"

Bobbie put down a red balloon as Jay appeared in the hallway. He didn't walk into the gym but stood beneath the door, studying the flying figure with the bow and arrow. He motioned to Bobbie to join him.

"Where've you been?" she asked. "I was afraid you weren't going to show."

Jay pointed up at the Cupid. "Look at that," he said grinning.

Bobbie looked at the figure, puzzled. Then she saw it. There, on the tip of the arrow, was a small sprig of mistletoe.

She backed away laughing. "Don't you guys have your holidays mixed up?"

"A Christmas leftover," Bill told her. "What better time to recycle it?"

The gym had been transformed into a giant valentine. Hearts and streamers hung from the walls, and red-and-white balloons trailed from the ceiling and basketball hoops. The decorating committee sat at a table in the corner, munching on the chocolate-chip cookies Nancy had brought.

"You're just in time," said Bill, as the rest of the group straggled in.

"Sorry we're late." Ron Stewart, a string-bean six-footer, flung his jacket over a chair and sat down. "My car was in the garage, and I had to pick it up."

Nancy giggled. "A real muscle man."

Ron glared at her. "Funny, Nancy."

"I thought so," she said. "Anyway, what do you think of our efforts?" She waved her arm at the decorations.

Linda Collins turned a critical eye on the gym. "Not bad. I like the big cupid over the door. He sets the theme for the party."

Ron laughed. "I took advantage of that when we came in. Right, Meg?" He raised his eyebrows. "Whose idea was that mistletoe? A touch of genius."

Meg Jones glowered at Ron. "Yeah, whose brainstorm was that?"

"I cannot tell a lie," Bill replied, grinning. "I saved it from a Christmas party my folks gave."

Nancy rolled her eyes but, for once, didn't say anything.

"So how's the entertainment coming?" George was constructing an intricate pyramid made of cookies.

Linda lifted one from the top and stared at it a moment. "I don't need this, but who can turn down a chocolate-chip cookie?" She munched in silence. "Now that I've added another five pounds, I suppose I should tell you we have a little problem with the entertainment. Angie Marconi was going to sing a couple of romantic songs during a break in the dancing, but she came down with laryngitis this morning. It's kind of late to come up with a replacement. Any suggestions?"

Bill took another cookie from George's pyramid. "How about relay races?"

"Right." Nancy stared thoughtfully at the table. "Wait a minute. Maybe Bobbie will do her clown act. None of us has actually seen Bubbles in person."

Bobbie couldn't hold back a gasp of surprise. "No, Nancy. Not at the dance!"

"Please, Bobbie," Nancy went on. "I think it's a good idea, even if it is mine. You'd only be onstage twenty minutes or so. What do the rest of you think?"

"Come on, Bobbie. We'd love to see your green-haired friend," Meg said.

"Well . . ." Ron drawled, "if we can't have a demonstration of how to change your oil, then I'm all for the clown."

Bobbie turned to Jay with a panicked expression. He grinned at her. "It looks as if you're outnumbered. Why not give it a try?"

"All right, all right," Bobbie gave in. "I'll do it. But I still don't think the Valentine's dance is the place for a clown act."

Bill tugged on her hair. "It's the perfect place. A little laughter never hurts."

Bobbie's doubts surfaced. "I can't perform without Jay," she told them. "We're a team."

Jay shook his head. "I can't do it this time, Bobbie. This is your school party. I'm just a stranger from East High."

She glared at him. "Thanks a lot, traitor."

"Good," Linda said quickly. "That's settled. Bobbie will be our entertainment break."

Nancy restacked her books and stood up, stretching. "I'm glad that's taken care of. I'm bushed. Let's call it quits."

Bobbie lingered at the table, ceremoniously arranging her books while the others filed out, laughing and talking noisily. Jay stood by, waiting. Finally Bobbie turned to face him.

"How could you go along with them?" she asked angrily. "I feel as if I've been pushed into performing. I don't want to go onstage as Bubbles. It's a school dance! And why do you think I should perform, when you don't want to?"

He reached out, his hand touching hers. "It's not that I don't want to. But don't you see, your friends want to watch *you*, to see for themselves why Bubbles is so special to you."

She shook her head. "I still don't see how I can dress in that crazy clown outfit and stumble onstage in front of everyone—even my teachers," she moaned. "I can't do it, Jay. I won't go to the dance." She felt a tear trickle down her cheek and sniffed loudly. If there was one thing she didn't want, it was for Jay to see her cry.

He turned her around to face him, gently erasing the tear with his thumb. "You have to go." His voice was a whisper. "You invited me, remember? And I'll be there right up front, cheering you on. OK?"

She looked up at him for a moment and slowly smiled. "How come you always know the right thing to say?"

He thought quietly for a minute. "It's a gift I have. You know I'm right."

"I guess so," she said as she nodded. "OK. I'll do it. I just hope I don't regret it."

The evening of the Valentine's Day dance was hectic. Bobbie dressed in a pale lilac formal, dabbed on a little lipstick and eye makeup, packed Bubbles's outfit and props into a suitcase, and waited in the living room for Jay to arrive. She paced nervously, her thoughts darting ahead to the performance in front of her friends. What if she wasn't funny? What if she was so nervous she couldn't remember her act?

Her mother glanced up from the needlepoint she was working on. "Calm down, Bobbie. This is a special night for you. Enjoy it."

Bobbie gave her mother a frantic look. "How can I, Mom? I'm afraid I'll make a fool of myself." She took a deep breath and let it out slowly. It didn't help. The butterflies were still dancing in her stomach. "Where is Jay, anyway? He's late." She paced back and forth in front of the fireplace.

Her father checked his watch. "He said he'd pick you up at seven, and it's only a quarter to. Sit down, or you'll wear a hole in the carpet."

Bobbie knew he was trying to get her to relax, but it didn't help. It was Jay's arrival, five minutes later, that finally put an end to her frantic pacing.

He wore a dark gray suit that made his hair seem even lighter than usual. Bobbie asked herself how she could keep forgetting how handsome he was. Just looking at him made her happy.

"Here," he said, shyly. He was holding out a white box. "I hope it's OK."

Bobbie opened the box, her eyes widening. "A white orchid. Oh, it's beautiful, Jay!" It was her first corsage. She promised herself that after the dance she would press it and keep it forever. "I'll wait until we get to school to pin it on," she said. "My coat would crush it."

Jay was smiling at her, and his blue eyes lit up as if he knew some secret.

"What is it?" she asked.

"Just wondering."

"Wondering what?"

"I was wondering if you knew how pretty you look tonight." He took her arm. "Come on, let's go to that dance."

Chapter Seven

A short time later, Bobbie and Jay joined the crowd in the Wilson High gym. A local DJ was playing a mix of rock and country, with an occasional slow dance slipped in.

Bobbie danced with George and Ron Stewart, but mostly she danced with Jay. During one slow, dreamy number, she glanced up to see a faraway look in his eyes. "You look a hundred miles away," she told him.

"No," he said, pulling her closer. "This is exactly where I want to be."

Midway through the evening, the DJ took his break, and everyone poured into the auditorium where the school jazz band was playing a brief set until Bubbles made her entrance. Reluctantly, Bobbie left Jay with Nancy and Bill and hurried backstage to dress for her act. *I can't believe I agreed to this,* she thought as she slipped off the lavender formal and put on the baggy clown suit. *They're not going to think I'm funny; they'll just think I'm insane.* She winced as she applied the cold, slippery greasepaint. Her hands felt clammy, and her stomach ached. For the fifth time that night, she wished she could escape to another planet.

Jeff West, who was acting as stagehand, gave her the entrance cue, and Bubbles stumbled onto the stage. A loud gasp went up from the audience, followed by laughter as she continued to stumble. She reached center stage, and the bright spotlight shone down on her. Without letting herself think, she began her juggling act. Sponge balls went flying into the band and audience—everywhere but where they were supposed to go. As she warmed up to her act, she forgot the audience. She heard the laughter after each act and wondered only briefly if her friends were laughing at her or at Bubbles the Clown. When she finally held up a sign reading THE END, applause and whistles rocked the room.

Bobbie was backstage, already lifting off the green wig, when she realized that her audience was still clapping, and like a rock-concert crowd demanding an encore, they were clapping in sync. "Guess you're not done," she said to her reflection in the mirror. With a grin at her own white face, she straightened the wig and reached into her suitcase for an out-of-shape hula hoop.

Onstage, Bobbie wiggled and squirmed her way into the hoop and tried desperately to spin it around her plump, padded waist. She felt as if the audience's laughter were carrying her. At last she bowed, blowing kisses to them all, and stumbled offstage.

Jay stood waiting backstage. "You did it, Bobbie!" he cried, swinging her around in his arms. "You had the audience in the palm of your hand. They loved you!"

"Are you sure?" Now that it was over, she was trembling. She still couldn't believe it.

"The guy next to me almost fell off his chair laughing." He ran his hand through the curly wig. "You've never been better."

Bobbie checked herself in the backstage mirror. Once again she was dressed in her lavender formal, looking exactly as she had when the evening started, and yet she knew something had changed.

Nancy met her at the refreshment table in the gym, hugging her. "You were terrific!"

Even Bill sounded unusually sincere. "I

never liked clown acts much, but you cracked me up."

George waited until the end of the dance to approach Bobbie. He stood for a moment, staring at her, then shook his head. "I can't believe that was you up there onstage," he said. "I have to admit you were good."

"You're not mad at me anymore? I mean, about math club and all?"

George grinned. "I guess I did give you a hard time, didn't I? I just felt kind of let down, and I couldn't understand how anyone could trade math for clowning. It makes a little more sense to me now."

"Well, you may not believe this," Bobbie told him, "but it wasn't an easy trade." Impulsively, she hugged him. "Thanks, George."

The rest of the evening Bobbie walked on air.

Later, at her door, under the soft glow of the porch light, she turned to Jay. "Thanks," she told him quietly, looking up into his eyes.

"For what?"

"Everything." A cold breeze tugged at her hair, and she brushed a wisp aside. "I never would have gone on with Bubbles tonight if it hadn't been for you."

He looked straight into her eyes for a moment, then lowered his glance. "It was nothing," he said, his voice husky.

"Hey, don't look so serious. Do you want to come in for a while? It's still pretty early."

Jay drew in a deep breath. "I don't know, Bobbie. I'm kind of mixed up," he told her wearily. "I still have a lot of practicing to do tonight."

She stared at him, puzzled. "You practice every night. What's wrong, anyway? Didn't you have a good time at the dance?"

"You know I did. It was great. You were terrific."

"Then come on in," she said, laughing. "We can find something to eat and watch a movie. Dad rented three good ones for the VCR. No one is home yet. My folks went to dinner and a show with friends."

Jay put his hands on her shoulders, shaking his head. "I have something to tell you, Bobbie. And I don't think you're going to like it." He let go of her and turned away, staring across the frost-covered lawn. "I don't know quite how to say it."

Bobbie suddenly felt the butterflies return. All the magic of the evening slipped away. She had never seen Jay look so serious. Was he going to tell her he had found someone he liked better? The thought made her sick. "Just say it." She swallowed hard, not sure she wanted to hear his next words.

Chapter Eight

Jay leaned forward, his lips brushing hers in a light kiss, and Bobbie was crushed that such a special moment was happening now. The kiss should have thrilled her, but instead it felt like goodbye. Bobbie pulled back, her eyes searching his face.

"You'd better come in," she said. "It's too cold to stand out here."

"OK," he said simply, following her inside to the living room.

"Now," she said, sitting down on the sofa, "what's the matter? You look positively miserable."

Jay said nothing. He stared at the blank TV.

Bobbie tried again. "Why don't you take off your coat and relax? I'll get us some soda."

"No, thanks," he said quietly, making no move to remove his jacket. Finally, he turned to face her. "I have something to tell you, Bobbie, and there's no easy way to say it." He gave a deep sigh. "I—I can't be part of the act any longer."

For a brief moment Bobbie thought he was teasing her, but the tone of his voice told her it was no joke. She stared at him a moment, not believing her ears. "What did you say?" she exclaimed, her voice shrill.

He looked down, unable to meet her eyes. "I have a chance to take private lessons from Theodore Milken, Bobbie. I don't know if you've heard of him, but he's one of the best banjo players in the country. He's going to be teaching here at the Eastman School of Music for the next few months." Jay's eyes brightened as he spoke. "He's also agreed to take on a few private students. I auditioned for him last week. I never thought he'd take me." He shrugged. "He phoned me tonight, just before the dance, to say he'll take me on as a pupil, starting right away. And it's going to take every minute that I'm not in school. I waited until now to tell you, so it wouldn't spoil the evening for you. I'm sorry about the act, Bobbie, but I'm glad about the lessons."

She knew he wanted her to understand, but at the moment all she could feel was a terrible numbness that quickly gave way to anger. One fact spun around and around in her brain. This was the end for Bubbles and Jay. Did that mean it was also the end for Bobbie and Jay? She swallowed hard, anger flashing in her eyes. "I—I don't know what to say. Why didn't you warn me? I didn't have any idea you were thinking of leaving the act."

His expression was troubled. "I wasn't sure, Bobbie. I didn't want to upset you if the lessons didn't work out. I'll miss our good times together, too." He reached out to tug at her bangs. "I'll miss Bubbles and her crazy green hair and even the egg she used to get all over me. But, I have to grab this chance. You know how important music is to me. Studying with Milken is like a dream I never believed would come true."

Bobbie huddled in the corner of the sofa. Tears stung her eyes and trickled slowly down her cheeks. She felt cold, as if the wind had suddenly blown open the door and swept through the room, and she shivered with the anger and resentment boiling inside her. "I think it's lousy!" she snapped. "Everything seemed so perfect." *Too perfect*, she thought bitterly. She should have known that nothing that good would last forever.

Jay's hands were on her shoulders, turning her to face him. "You can go on without me in the act, Bobbie. You proved that tonight."

"You set me up," she said quietly.

"I what?"

"That's why you wanted me to go on alone tonight. You wanted me to perform solo, even though you knew I didn't want to do the act in front of my friends, just so you could tell me you were leaving."

"That's not true," Jay said. "No one set you up. I didn't even know—"

"Well, it doesn't make it any easier," she went on furiously. "Tonight was one twenty-minute show. I can't do the act at hospitals the way we did." She stood up, searching her pocket for a tissue.

Jay reached out, gently lifting her chin so that she had to look at him. "Why can't you? You saw how much the kids love Bubbles. I'm just an added attraction. You'll do fine as a solo act. Come on, Bobbie, be glad for me. I'm really excited about these lessons with a master. Not everyone gets a chance like this."

Her stomach churned until she felt almost sick. Not once had she thought that their partnership might come to an end. Since that day at Amy's birthday party, Jay had become the most important person in her life. And now the act itself seemed as much a part of her as breathing.

"How can you just say this is the end?" she asked, sniffing. Even though Jay hadn't said so, it sounded to her as if that night also marked the end of their relationship. She clenched her fists and her anger flared. When he put his hands on her arms she pulled away, glaring at him.

"Just go," she shouted, fighting tears. "Take your stupid banjo lessons and go away. Who needs you anyway? It's better like this." She felt the unwanted tears fill her eyes. "I don't care if I ever see you again."

Before he could utter another word, Bobbie turned and ran to her room. She heard the front door slam, followed shortly by the sound of Jay's car speeding up the road.

Sniffing, she sat down on the edge of her bed, absently fingering the chintz bedspread. She felt empty and suddenly more alone than she had ever been before.

"Oh, no," she moaned. Her mother's voice called up the stairs, "We're home, Bobbie. How was the dance? Come down and tell us about it."

Bobbie grabbed a tissue from the box on her nightstand and blew her nose loudly. She didn't feel like facing anyone right then, least of all her mother. "It was OK," she called back. "I'll tell you about it tomorrow. I'm really tired." The excuse was weak, but for then she wanted to be alone. She lay across her bed, the orchid corsage crushed against the bedspread. She reached down and yanked it off, throwing it across the room. "I hate you, Jay Hartwell," Bobbie sobbed into the bedspread. "You're mean and selfish."

She ignored the insistent ringing of her bedside phone until she couldn't stand the sound another second. Anger echoed in her voice as she answered, expecting to hear Jay's voice, apologizing.

Instead, Nancy's cheery voice greeted her. "I know it's late, but I figured you'd be up. I know I'm too wide-awake to sleep. I thought I'd call and tell you how much I enjoyed Bubbles," she chattered on. "No kidding, Bobbie, you were really funny. Everyone I talked to loved the act. Wasn't the dance great?" She drew in a deep breath, then continued, "I think you and Jay were the best-looking couple there. You're lucky, you know. A lot of the girls think so."

Bobbie scowled into the phone. "That's a matter of opinion," she muttered, sitting up, propping a pillow against the headboard on her bed and making herself comfortable. "I'm glad you called, Nancy. I need to talk." As long as they had known each other, they had shared secrets and feelings no one else knew about. It was a relief now to tell her friend about the disastrous ending to the evening.

Nancy listened sympathetically while Bobby told her about Jay's news and her own angry reaction. "I really lost my temper," Bobbie admitted.

"I don't blame you." Nancy sounded annoyed. "It was a rotten thing to do. He could have at least warned you that he might leave the act. He's probably known for ages. I swear, boys can be such jerks." Her voice softened. "Look, Bobbie, don't give up Bubbles. I never thought I'd say this, but you have a special talent. Jay has nothing to do with that. You invented that clown before you even met him."

"I know," Bobbie said. "But it won't be fun without him, Nance. I really like him, and I thought he liked me." She sighed. "I know I'll never see him again."

"You'll get over him," Nancy told her. "George will see to that."

Bobbie moaned. She knew Nancy had meant to be funny, but she didn't feel much like laughing at the moment. "Keep it quiet, will you? Don't tell anyone for a while, OK?" Bobbie pleaded. "I don't think I'm ready to handle a lot of dumb questions."

"No one else will know," her friend told her. "I promise."

Minutes later Bobbie had to recount the events of the evening again, when her mother came upstairs to see what was wrong.

"I can understand why you're upset, Bobbie," Mrs. Reese told her. "It's a shame it had to happen right now. I imagine Jay feels bad about it, too."

Bobbie picked up her pillow and punched it. "He should. I never want to see him again." She turned to face her mother, sitting beside her on the bed. "Mom, do you think that's wrong?"

"Never is a long time," Mrs. Reese said quietly. "I'm sure you will be less angry in time."

"You sound as if you're on Jay's side."

Her mother shook her head. "I'm not on anyone's side, Bobbie. I can see why you're hurt, but Jay obviously didn't know about the lessons until recently, and he didn't want to ruin your evening."

"Well, he *did*." Bobbie looked at the white corsage lying on the floor. "He's ruined everything."

"Things will look better tomorrow," Mrs. Reese said. "You'd better turn in now."

It wasn't easy to slip into sleep that night. Bobbie tossed and turned, remembering Jay's final words and her own angry response. Outside, the wind began to blow, whipping the falling snow into drifts, but Bobbie was hardly aware of it. A storm just as intense raged within her. What would happen to Bubbles without Jay? And how could she have said goodbye to the first boy she had ever really loved? Hours later she fell into a troubled sleep, still not knowing the answers.

In the days following the Valentine's Day dance, Bobbie tried to push the next scheduled performance out of her mind. She and Jay had usually performed on weekends, but this one was going to be an after-school party; it meant that Bubbles's routine would have to be different. Of course, Bubbles's routine was going to be very different without Jay. Bobbie wondered if there was still time to bow out of the appearance; she could come up with a reason that sounded logical. She tried to imagine entertaining a roomful of nursing-home patients all by herself, and a chill crept up her spine. There was no way she could go onstage alone.

And Bobbie would have come up with an excellent excuse if Mrs. Alderson, the nursing home supervisor, hadn't caught her off guard. She had answered the phone on Tuesday, sure that it was Nancy.

"Bobbie," Mrs. Alderson began, "I talked to

Jay briefly, and he explained that he won't be able to play his banjo for us. But I've assured the seniors that Bubbles will be there. Will you need a ride? If so, I can come by and pick you up at three tomorrow."

Tomorrow, Bobbie thought with a sinking heart.

"Do you need a ride?" Mrs. Alderson repeated.

"No thanks," she said at last. "I'll see if my dad will leave work early and drive me. He's good about things like that."

After Mrs. Alderson hung up, Bobbie sat on her bed, scowling, still holding the phone but oblivious of the insistent dial tone. Why hadn't she given the woman an excuse, any excuse? That she had to visit her Aunt Julia in Niagara Falls, or take Amy to the library— anything! Now she was committed to perform.

The shrill tone suddenly coming from the receiver brought Bobbie back to the present. She hung up the phone, shaking her head at her own absentmindedness. She wished her stomach would stop its nervous rumblings.

Chapter Nine

That evening, before supper, Bobbie went to the living room to talk to her father. She found him sitting in his favorite reclining chair, doing a crossword puzzle. She waited patiently until he filled in a word, then made her request. "I hate to ask you to chauffeur me again, Dad. I know you're tired when you get home from work, but this is a special request. I have an afternoon show tomorrow at the nursing home."

Mr. Reese set the puzzle book on the table beside his chair. "I can leave Ed Lane in charge at the store." His face broke into a smile as he saw his daughter's worried expression. "Hey, a dad likes to feel needed," he told her. "It will be like old times, driving you. I can remember when every day I was ferrying you and Nancy to meetings, or basketball games, or school plays." He nodded his head thoughtfully. "To be truthful, your old dad was a bit jealous when the boys started to drive you around."

Bobbie couldn't imagine her father jealous of anyone, but his words made her feel good. She leaned over to kiss his cheek. "You're the greatest, Dad."

The following day, as soon as she got home from school, she dressed in her clown outfit and waited for her father to pick her up. A light misty rain was falling as they drove across town. Bobbie shivered, feeling cold right to the bone. "I'd rather have snow," she mumbled, reaching over to turn on the heater.

Her father glanced at her, puzzled. "There'll be plenty more snow before March blows in, and there's certainly enough of it around now. For someone who likes the white stuff, your mood isn't the best. What was the motto you started out with? 'Bubbles chases troubles'?"

Bobbie sighed. "You're right, Dad. I'm just nervous about this appearance, that's all. It's my first time doing the whole show myself. I'm not sure I can do it."

Mr. Reese drove into the nursing-home parking lot and stopped at the door. "Of course you can do it," he said, thumping his hand on the steering wheel for emphasis. "We Reeses never give up. Look, I have a few errands to run while you're entertaining the patients, but I'll be back in about an hour to pick you up." He gave her a wide smile that crinkled the corners of his dark eyes. "We'll stop at the Burger Barn on the way home and pick up our supper. How does that sound?"

Bobbie squared her shoulders. "Terrific," she told him lightly. "I'll be starved by then." She blew him a kiss. "See you later, Dad."

She entered the home and hurried along, as fast as her clumsy shoes would allow, toward the recreation room where a birthday party was already in progress.

"We've been waiting for you, Bubbles," said a stooped old woman near the door.

Tall, efficient-looking Mrs. Alderson hurried across the room to meet her. "Come in, Bobbie. We're all set up for you. The stage is yours." She raised her hand and her voice. "Ladies and gentlemen, you all remember Bubbles the Clown. She's come back again today to help us celebrate Mamie Olson's ninety-ninth birthday. Let's give her a warm welcome."

Bobbie looked at the rows of wheelchair patients and those seated on straight-backed cafeteria chairs. Not one seat was empty. For a moment she felt a nervous fluttering in her stomach, but the applause urged her onstage, skipping and whistling her own music. When she stumbled and heard the chuckles of the elderly patients, she went into an impromptu act of blowing up balloons to throw one at a time. They were supposed to go out in the audience but instead fell to the floor at her feet. Finally, with a discouraged droop of her shoulders, she clopped down off the stage and handed the balloons to the first few people she came to. Then, bowing, she returned to the stage to do her hula-hoop bit. This time she became stuck in the plastic hoop and struggled to wriggle it over her plump body. The seniors laughed, and she felt a sharp pang—she missed Jay. Turning her mind to juggling the sponges, she forced herself to concentrate, forced herself to forget him.

The act was a hit. When Bobbie had exhausted her bag of tricks, she bowed and blew kisses to the audience. A feeling of accomplishment welled up inside her. The applause she was hearing then was just as enthusiastic as it had been when Jay performed with her. He'd been right, after all. She could do the act alone.

*　　*　　*

In the week that followed Bobbie performed solo at a birthday party for another friend of Amy's and put on a show at a local nursery school.

February finally eased into March, but winter hung on with cold, biting winds, snow squalls, and flurries. It was one of Bobbie's rare free Saturdays, and Nancy had talked her into spending the afternoon at the mall. They went to the record shop first, checking out the latest albums and VCR tapes.

Eventually, they wound up in a little boutique where Bobbie bought a bright red sweater with a white heart on one sleeve.

"It's a morale booster," she told Nancy. "Besides, it was half price, and I look good in red." What she didn't say was that the heart was for Jay.

After stopping in the card store to buy stationery, they sat down to enjoy cold glasses of freshly squeezed orange juice and watch the people walk by.

Nancy played with the straw in her glass, rattling the ice cubes. "So, have you heard anything from Jay?" she asked, finally.

Bobbie sipped her drink a moment before answering. "To be honest, every time the phone rings I hope it's him, but it never is." She drew in a deep breath and exhaled slowly.

"My feelings are all jumbled up, Nance. I think about the good times we had, and then I remember the way I felt when he told me he was quitting the act." She shrugged. "I guess it's over for good. I'm getting along OK with the show without him. I really am." She bit her lip, knowing the tears would come at any minute. "I still miss him, Nancy. I really miss him."

"I can understand that." Nancy put an arm around her friend's shoulders. "If Bill ever left me, I'd be a basket case. We've been going steady for such a long time."

"I don't think you'll have to worry about Bill. I can see you two getting married after graduation and living happily ever after. You're lucky, you know."

"I know. Bill's terrific. But don't you give up. You may see Jay again," Nancy told her quietly. "Anyway, I think it's great that you're going on with the clown act by yourself."

Bobbie smiled. "It isn't always easy. Sometimes I enjoy doing the act; other times I wish Jay were there to lend a hand. His music was special. And it used to feel so good just working with him." She tipped her cup back and caught an ice cube. Bobbie gave a long sigh. "You must get tired of hearing about my clown act and all my problems.

Remember when we were little, how simple things were? Why can't they be like that now?"

Nancy stood up and laughed. "If you find the answer to that one, let me know. Bill says I make things complicated. Maybe I do. Maybe we both do. Actually, looking back, I don't think things were always that great when we were younger. We just had smaller problems, that's all." She grinned at Bobbie. "Come on, let's cut the gloom and check out the bookstore before we leave. I hear there's a neat new series out about college life." She clicked her teeth. "Lots of romance."

They walked down the long, carpeted mall to the bookstore, where they each bought one of the new paperbacks. Then they hurried out to the road to wait for the bus home.

Bobbie had five long, uneventful days at school before her next Saturday afternoon performance. There was plenty of time to think about Jay, and about Bubbles. Her talk with Nancy at the mall had made her realize just how lonely she was. Doubts crept into her mind. Could she go on and on performing alone? Maybe she ought to quit and return to the math club. There were times when she missed the group and the challenge of the problems. She had changed her life for Jay.

She could change it back for herself. Maybe then, with no Bubbles act to remind her, she would actually forget about Jay. But whatever she decided, she would definitely do the show at Strong Memorial on Saturday.

Saturday was cold, clear, and sunny. Just right for the hospital party. Bobbie kept the children laughing in the solarium on the pediatric ward. There were a few new faces in the audience and some familiar ones. Bobbie saw Wendy in her favorite spot, her wheelchair away from the others. She found herself playing directly to the girl. When Wendy finally smiled at a card trick and actually giggled when she juggled a banana, an orange, and a grape, Bobbie felt encouraged. At the end of the show, Bobbie clomped down from the platform where she performed and made her way to the side of the sun-filled room.

"Hi, Bubbles." A little boy in a wheelchair tugged at her sleeve. "I think you're funny."

Bobbie ruffled the boy's red hair. "I'm glad to hear that."

A girl with pig-tails and a bandage around her forehead waved in Bobbie's face. "We love you. We want you to come here every day," she said. "Come for my birthday next week.

I'm going to be six. My stitches come out then."

Bobbie smiled. "We'll see," she promised. She made her way to where Wendy sat. When she reached the child, she stooped down in front of her and took her hands. "What about you, Wendy? Do you want Bubbles to come again?"

A pair of wide brown eyes stared at her, and a hint of a smile touched the corners of Wendy's mouth. Silently, she shrugged her thin shoulders. Then her smile widened. She squeezed Bobbie's hands tightly. "I love you, too," she said in an almost inaudible whisper.

Bobbie leaned over to kiss Wendy's cheek. She knew she had tears in her eyes, but she didn't care.

"I'll come back again, Wendy," she promised. "Maybe we can have a long talk." She reached out to smooth a curl back from the girl's forehead.

Bobbie stood up, waved again to the children, and made her way out into the hall. She felt like singing.

One of the nurses stopped her in the hallway. "You performed a miracle today, you know. Wendy has been here over two months and hasn't said a word the whole time. Her parents divorced just before Christmas, and Wendy hasn't been able to accept it. It's been

easier for her to retreat into her own world."
She put her hand on Bobbie's arm. "Keep it
up, won't you? You're doing a wonderful
service."

"Thank you," Bobbie said. "I'll come back
whenever you want me to. I'm so happy about
Wendy finally talking."

And she was. As Bobbie removed her makeup and changed into her clothes, she kept
hearing Wendy's words.

She noticed a phone near the elevator and
paused a moment. The urge to tell Jay about
Wendy was strong, and the urge to hear his
voice was even stronger. Bobbie stepped into
the booth, her hand trembling as she depos-
ited her money and dialed Jay's number. The
droning sound of the busy signal greeted her.

A short time later Bobbie hurried across
the lobby, where her father waited for her.

"How did it go?" Mr. Reese asked her, taking the suitcase from her hand. "Did the kids
still get a chuckle out of Bubbles?"

"Dad, it was great. You should have been
there. Remember my telling you about Wendy,
the little girl who never talked? Today she
spoke to me, and it was because of Bubbles.
The nurse said it was a real breakthrough for
her."

Her father opened the door for her, smiling. "That, my dear, is what clowning is all about."

"Lately I've thought about quitting the clown act," Bobbie admitted. "I guess I'll go on with it for a while longer—'till the kids get sick of Bubbles."

"They won't," Mr. Reese said, shaking his head. "You'll see."

Chapter Ten

Bobbie was relieved to find that Bubbles had no scheduled appearances for the next couple of weeks. She needed time alone to think.

It was Bobbie's favorite time of the year. The snows were melting, and there was a promise of spring in the air. The pussy willow tree in the side yard had puffy gray buds, and hyacinths had just poked their green heads out of the ground. Bobbie took long walks, listening to the sparrows call. More often than not, she thought of Jay and how much she missed him. It seemed an eternity since the fateful evening of the Valentine's Day dance. She had relived that night dozens of times in her mind, searching for even a slight hint of what was to come. She and Jay had been happy at the dance, and if anything, the early part of the evening seemed to bring them closer together. Their breakup had come like a violent explosion—sudden and final. The knowledge that she was partly to blame for the breakup didn't help. She knew she had hurt Jay by her outburst. But, he had hurt her first by leaving her to go on alone with the act they had shared. No matter how many times she thought about that evening, she could see no solution to the problem. And there was no forgetting it. Time, she knew, was the only answer.

On a sunny day in the middle of March, Bobbie waited in front of school for Nancy. She was watching a flock of mourning doves nibble at the bread crumbs someone had dropped beside the sidewalk. The grass was starting to green up, she noticed, and tiny buds were showing on some trees. Winter had seemed especially long, and she was glad to have it over.

"Hey, Bobbie." George's voice startled her. "Want a ride home? I've got my father's car today." He dangled the key under her nose.

She turned to face him, smiling. "Sure. Bill will be driving Nancy home as usual. She won't miss me."

The white sedan still had that special "new" smell. Bobbie sank into the plush red seat. "This is nice," she said, feeling the soft material. She turned to face him, as they drove onto the road. "How is math club? I hear things are looking up, and the team is winning again. I told you I wouldn't be missed."

George concentrated on his driving. "I wouldn't exactly say that. It's taken us a long time to break that losing streak. I've been doing a lot of extra studying, so have the others. We're determined not to let East High beat us in the final competition."

She felt a brief pang of guilt but brushed it aside. They drove in silence for a few moments. Bobbie ran her hand over the back of the seat and decided to level with her friend. "Sometimes I miss it, George."

"You can always come back," he told her, easing up to a stop sign and looking both ways before driving on. "I hate these four-way stop signs," he muttered through his teeth.

"You and my mom," she said, laughing.

He patted the dashboard gently. "Driving this car makes me jumpy," he told her. "If I get one small dent in it my name will be capital M-U-D, and my father will ground me for eternity."

"You're a good driver," she told him. "You

don't have anything to worry about." She thought of Jay and his battered car. One more dent wouldn't matter much there. The upholstery was worn and spotted, but that hadn't mattered either. She had loved to ride with Jay. George stopped at a traffic light, and she quickly turned her attention back to him. "Anyway, I've thought a couple of times about returning to math club. Would you believe, when I get a few days without a party or show, I actually find myself looking up problems in my sister's old college algebra book and working them out to keep from getting rusty."

George ventured a hasty look in her direction. "You're kidding me."

She shook her head, smiling.

"I'm sorry about the way things worked out between you and Jay." George's voice was quiet. "I mean it, Bobbie. I know how much doing the act with Jay meant to you. But you're doing OK on your own, aren't you?"

She sighed. "Yeah, I guess so."

George stopped in front of a small restaurant, parallel parking effortlessly. Bobbie smiled. George did everything right, which could actually get pretty boring. But that day, with spring hovering near, she was glad to be with him. He was a good friend, and when he decided to relax, he could be fun. "How about a soda or a shake or something?" he asked her, opening the door.

She followed him up the walk to the restaurant, aptly nicknamed the Noise Box. The booths were already filled with the after-school crowd. In one corner a huge old-fashioned jukebox blared out the latest rock tunes.

George ordered two tall root-beer floats, and they sat listening to the music. A slow ballad played above the chatter, and Bobbie winced, remembering how she and Jay had danced to that song at the Valentine's Day dance. The memory of that dance, of being in Jay's arms, hurt more than she would have expected. She drank her float quickly, finishing just as George muttered a low, "Uh, oh—don't look up, Bobbie. It's him."

"Him who?" She looked up quickly and saw Jay enter the restaurant and make his way to a back table. Her heart pounded at the sight of him. He wore a gray blue turtleneck sweater and a denim jacket; his hair was longer, a little wilder.

Bobbie stood up, ready to go back and talk to him, to tell him she was sorry she had been such an idiot. But Jay sat down across from an attractive dark-haired girl, smiling as if he'd known her for years.

Bobbie kept her voice carefully neutral. "Let's go, George. I have to get home." This was not the time or place to cry, and she could already feel the wetness in her eyes. She managed to stay calm until she got outside and then made a mad dash for the car. She got in, nervously tapping her fingers on the dashboard while she waited for George. It seemed forever before he came out and slid behind the wheel.

"I had to pay the check," he said apologetically. "Sorry it took so long."

They didn't talk on the ride to Bobbie's house. To his credit, George seemed to realize she needed to be left alone. Out of politeness she asked him to come in for a while, hoping in her heart he would refuse. George stared at her thoughtfully, as if trying to read her mind, and his expression of doubt made her feel guilty. He was a good guy, and he meant well. Bobby sighed. Maybe company would do her good. If she were alone she would only mope and think about Jay and the dark-haired girl. "It's OK," she told George, giving him a smile. "The cookie jar is full of homemade chocolate-chip cookies."

Mrs. Reese found them in the kitchen. "It's good to see you again, George," she said, sounding mildly surprised.

He pushed his glasses up on his nose. "It's good to be here, Mrs. Reese. Bobbie said you baked cookies, and I couldn't pass them up."

Mrs. Reese nodded, looking pleased. "You know where I keep them, just help yourself." She pulled a note from her pocket. "Bobbie, you missed a phone call from a woman at Strong Hospital. She said you promised to perform at their annual Welcome Spring party Sunday afternoon for the patients in the women's surgical ward. She wanted to remind you and asked if you'd need a ride."

Bobbie moaned, slapping her hand to her forehead. "Oh, no! I forgot to put that party on my calendar. How could I be so stupid. This is Friday already."

Her mother laughed. "You've been on the go so much lately, I'm not surprised you forgot. You'd better call her back as soon as you can."

"I will." Bobbie turned to George. "Would you like to come to the party? You could see the great clown in action."

"Me? To a party for sick women?" George shook his head. "No, thanks. I hate hospitals."

Bobbie sighed. *And green-haired clowns.* She had an idea George would rather slay a dragon than be seen with a freckle-nosed, floppy-shoed clown. "No problem," she told him. "I just thought I'd ask. Come on, let's eat. Those cookies are getting stale."

That Sunday Bobbie's parents drove her to the hospital. "Just give a call when you're ready to come home," her father told her. "We can be here in fifteen minutes."

"Thanks, Dad. You're the greatest."

She hurried inside and clomped down the long, sparkling clean hallway to the surgical ward. A sudden gnawing feeling of loneliness swept over her.

An elderly ambulatory patient stopped to speak to her. "You probably don't remember me," the woman said. "I saw you and that handsome young man who played the banjo when you put on a show in the children's ward in January. My little grandson was a patient then. My, but he loved that silly clown of yours."

"I'm glad," Bobbie said politely.

"You're such a perky clown. We're all looking forward to today's program," the woman said, shuffling past to her room. "Laughter is better than medicine."

Her words gave Bobbie a needed boost. She stood outside the patients' spacious lounge, watching the nurses and aides push the wheelchairs of those who couldn't walk. Some of the women looked seriously ill. Could she be funny when she looked into the faces of people in pain? Bobbie shivered at the thought.

Miss Danielson, the head nurse on the ward, introduced Bobbie, and there was no more time to think. She went on, and did her usual act. An old upright piano took up a corner of the stage, and Bobbie sat down to give a rousing rendition of "Chopsticks" before falling off the piano bench. Quickly she jumped up, patting her green hair and dusting off her clown suit. Applause filled the room, and Bobbie curtsied her thanks. She was pleased when those serious faces broke into smiles during her juggling routine. Once again Bubbles left her audience exhilarated.

Miss Danielson met her outside the lounge. "I have a request, Bobbie. I wonder if you would visit a heart patient who wasn't well enough to attend the show. I think it would please her."

"Sure," Bobbie said, wondering how she could entertain in a small room.

Miss Danielson looked relieved. "I was afraid you might say no. After all, you just did a strenuous show, and you must be tired. But, Mrs. Trent is very special, Bobbie. She's been here a long time, and I think it would be a real tonic for her if you would do a small part of your act at her bedside."

"I'll do my best," Bobbie assured her, picking out a few choice props.

Miss Danielson led the way down the hall to the last door. Bobbie stumbled when she entered Mrs. Trent's room and walked to her bedside. The pale-faced woman looked alarmed. Undaunted, Bubbles went into a few of her usual tricks, using her deck of cards, her sponge juggling balls, and the hula hoop. She felt out of place in the small, sterile room, as if she were performing for herself alone. Mrs. Trent remained silent and still. For a time Bobbie thought she had drifted into sleep. But when she ended her act, doing a floppy-shoed jig, the woman stretched out her thin, bony hand. Bobbie forgot to be the clown. She clasped the hand in hers, shivering at the coldness. A faint smile tugged at the corners of Mrs. Trent's pale lips as she whispered, "Thank you."

"That's one of the few times she's smiled since she arrived here, Bobbie," Miss Danielson told her when they left the room. "She's been very, very ill."

Bobbie felt strange the rest of the day. She couldn't erase Mrs. Trent's thin, pale face from her mind. She had never seen anyone so desperately ill before.

In the car on the way home she told her parents about Mrs. Trent. "It felt good to be able to give her a few minutes of the act, but I felt like crying the whole time. I don't know," she said, feeling more and more confused. "Maybe I'm not cut out to be around really sick people. Maybe it's time I quit—"

"Give it a lot of thought," her mother advised her.

Bobbie moaned. "I have. I am."

As they rode on she stared out the window, watching the familiar springtime scenes. Men and women worked in their yards, raking the winter's debris. Children rode bikes, skated, and tossed balls. It was supposed to be a good time, a time of awakening. Why did she feel so gloomy, so confused? Sometimes she had the feeling it would have been better if she had never dug the clown outfit out of the attic trunk. Then she wouldn't have this problem. And, she wouldn't have met Jay and wouldn't be so miserable without him.

"I hate this feeling," she mumbled. "It's like nothing will ever be right again."

"It will be," her mother told her gently. "You've had an emotionally draining day. You'll see it differently tomorrow."

"I hope so." A tear trickled down Bobbie's cheek, touching her lips. It tasted salty, and she brushed it aside. Briefly she wished she could turn back the clock and be seven or eight years old again. She sighed, remembering the day at the mall when she and Nancy had talked about being little kids again. She tried to think of one of her childhood tragedies and felt a faint smile tug at her mouth. A broken spoke on her bicycle when she wanted to ride to the park with Nancy had seemed devastating. And, she remembered a Valentine's Day long ago when every girl in the class but her had gotten cards from a freckle-faced little boy named Willis. Her heart had been broken. But by the following day she had fully recovered.

She shook her head. The crazy confusion she was feeling now was probably just another stage she'd grow out of. But why did it seem that it would never end?

Chapter Eleven

Bobbie hunched over her desk in study hall. She was trying to read the first act of *A Midsummer Night's Dream* for English when a voice over the public address system blared out:

"Will Bobbie Reese please report to the office as soon as possible?"

Several heads turned to look at her, and she felt herself blush. Nancy, seated at the desk next to her, leaned over to whisper, "What have you done now?"

Bobbie shrugged. "Nothing, I hope." She left her book open on the desk. "If I'm not back in ten minutes, send out a rescue team."

Bobbie hurried down the hall to the office. Mrs. Trumble, the principal's stern-faced secretary, who seemed to be in charge of everything, motioned to her to come in and sit down. Bobbie made her way through the narrow office to Mrs. Trumble's cluttered desk.

"Sit down, Bobbie," Mrs. Trumble said.

Bobbie did as she was told, her stomach churning the way it often did when she was nervous.

Mrs. Trumble stared at her desk a moment, pushed her glasses up on her nose, and glanced briefly at Bobbie. The phone on her desk rang, and she reached to answer it, saying, "I'll be with you in a minute, Bobbie."

Bobbie clasped her hands in her lap. Why did Mrs. Trumble want to see her, she wondered. Was the school unhappy about her putting so much time into her clown act? That could be it, but she had seen to it that her marks hadn't gone down. She glanced around the office, while Mrs. Trumble's voice droned into the phone. Mr. Melrose, the principal, was on the phone in the office. She could see him through the glass divider, leaning back in his chair and tapping his pen on the desk as he talked. Across from where Bobbie sat, two older women were busy typing. There was one familiar face in the room. Jenny Lewis, a senior, was at work on the computer. Bobbie watched her a moment. Maybe George was right. Running the computer looked as if it might be fun. Maybe she should look into the course next semester. George would be glad to tell her about floppy disks, disk drives, menus, commands, and things like that.

After what seemed an eternity, Mrs. Trumble hung up the phone and looked over her glasses at Bobbie. "I'm sorry that took so long," she said apologetically, her thin lips easing into a smile and transforming her usually stern face. Bobbie felt immediate relief. If anything were drastically wrong, Mrs. Trumble would never waste an ounce of energy in a smile.

"I've been going over your grades," Mrs. Trumble continued. "I see that your math marks are still the highest in your class, which brings me to our offer. We need another student here in the office to help with the bookkeeping on special student projects, such as orchestra and chorus funds, money for school-related trips, and so forth. We're setting up a new system to be handled strictly by the students themselves. We need someone dependable, someone we can count on." She paused, peering over her glasses. "We thought of you. I'm sure the experience will be valuable. Are you interested, Bobbie? You can work during your free periods, and for an hour or two after school. As I said, the experience will be beneficial to someone like yourself. You do plan to go on with your math, don't you?"

Bobbie was caught off guard. Math was fun; she enjoyed figuring out difficult problems, the way her father enjoyed doing crossword puzzles. But at the moment, she wasn't at all sure she wanted to make it her entire life. She hadn't given the future that much thought. After all, she was only a sophomore. She nibbled at her lower lip, her thoughts spinning crazily. If she accepted the job, she would definitely have to pack away her Bubbles outfit. It would be an easy way to put an end to the act. She studied her fingers a moment. What would Jay think? She sighed, hunching her shoulders. What did it matter? She was never going to see him again anyway. Jay Hartwell lived in another world, and his silence made it obvious she wasn't welcome in that world.

Bobbie looked up and met Mrs. Trumble's stare. "Can I think about it, Mrs. Trumble? You know I entertain at hospitals quite often, so I don't have much free time."

The secretary nodded. "I've heard about your clown act, and I realize that working here would take several hours a week. Perhaps you wouldn't have as much time to go out and entertain at parties. But please think about it seriously and let me know as soon as you can. We have another young lady in mind if you don't accept the position." Mrs. Trumble stood up, offering a faint smile. "Have a good day, Bobbie."

That was it. The meeting had been short and sweet, and, like it or not, Bobbie found herself faced with another decision. It was obvious that Mrs. Trumble didn't consider her Bubbles act nearly as important as student funds. Bobbie thought about that as she hurried back to study hall to collect her books and join the stampede of students heading toward the lunchroom. She spied Nancy at a table in the corner and elbowed her way through a group waiting to find a place in the cafeteria line.

The second she sat down, Nancy wanted an explanation. "OK, Bobbie, why were you summoned to the big chief's office?"

Bobbie filled her in quickly on the job offer.

"It sounds great." Nancy opened her lunch bag and pulled out a carton of yogurt and a plastic spoon. "It will look good on your record and give you a reference when you go job hunting."

Bobbie munched a bite of apple, barely tasting it. "I guess so. I didn't think of that. I'm just mixed up, Nancy. You know how I hate making decisions."

"Yeah, but this one might be good for you.

You said you aren't sure you want to go clowning much longer anyway." Nancy shrugged. "If they offered me a job in the office, I'd grab it. Think of the prestige. Lauren Jackson has been dying to get an after-school job for two years. She'll turn green if you end up working there." Nancy sighed. "I might turn a shade of chartreuse myself. It could be fantastic. Sooner or later you'd get to see everyone in the school. What a way to meet new guys when they transfer here—or seniors checking on fund-drive money. This job definitely has a lot of possibilities."

Bobbie finished her apple and picked at half of a tuna sandwich. She knew her friend's words were meant to encourage her, but in fact they had the opposite effect. Right then she had no desire to meet new boys; she only wanted Jay. Nancy, of all people, should understand that.

"I'll think about it over the weekend and let Mrs. Trumble know Monday morning," Bobbie said flatly.

Nancy scraped the bottom of the yogurt carton, shaking her head. "Wish I could help."

Bobbie scowled. "Nobody can help, Nancy. It's my problem, and I guess it'll have to be my decision." She wadded her lunch bag into a ball and tossed it into a nearby barrel. Her frown vanished. "Hey, did you see that shot?

130

Not bad. Maybe I should forget clowning *and* the office job and try out for basketball. That would solve my problems."

Nancy glared at her, and Bobbie laughed. "It was a joke. I wanted to change the subject. OK?"

"OK. Come on, let's get to social studies class before we're late."

Bobbie moaned. "You're right. One minute past the bell, and Ms. Stone will be giving out surprise quizzes."

They gathered up their books and joined the crowd filing out the door into the hall.

Bobbie decided not to mention the office job to her parents until she reached a definite decision. On Saturday when Ellen and Amy came over after a shopping trip in town, Bobbie quietly left the house, heading straight for her favorite refuge—the small park a short block from the Reese home. Usually she loved to play with Amy, but that day she needed time alone, away from the child's boundless energy and nonstop chatter. It was time to decide whether she should take the office job and return the clown outfit to the attic, or go on with the act, without Jay.

The park was a peaceful haven. Green grass pushed aside the dull brown of winter. The crocuses were flowering, and Bobbie knew it was just a matter of a few warm, sunny days until the park would be ablaze with color. She sat down on a wooden bench near the fountain, watching a flock of pigeons eat bread scattered by an elderly man and woman. One pigeon walked with overlapping feet and seemed to stumble now and then as he walked, pecking for the crumbs. Bobbie giggled. He reminded her of Bubbles and her floppy shoes. She sighed, thinking of the act she had done so often. She liked that klutzy clown. She couldn't deny that.

"OK, Bobbie, it's honesty time," she muttered. "There's no one here to help you. You're on your own, so make up your mind what you're going to do." She chewed her lower lip thoughtfully.

There were two facts to consider. She liked Bubbles, and she liked math. *But,* the Bubbles act wasn't the same without Jay—nothing was. The job at school might help her get her mind off the past. She stood up, sighing. The answer was there, plain as the fountain in front of her. First thing Monday morning she would tell Mrs. Trumble she accepted the job in the school office. It would be a new beginning, and right then that was what she needed. She couldn't mope around being miserable forever. How many times while she was growing up had her father told her,

"Things change, Bobbie. Nothing stays the same forever." She had never known what he meant until that very moment.

She squared her shoulders, took several deep breaths of the fresh spring air, and headed back toward home. Her decision came back to spin around in her brain as she walked, and slowly her footsteps began to drag. Why, if she had made her decision, didn't she feel happy about it? What was the matter with her, anyway?

"Blast you, Jay Hartwell," she exclaimed, startling an entire flock of pigeons into flight. "It's all your fault."

Chapter Twelve

On Sunday morning Bobbie woke to the sun streaming in through her bedroom windows. A robin sang in the big blue spruce tree in the backyard, and somewhere far off a cardinal whistled to its mate. Bobbie slipped out of bed, showered, dressed in jeans and a light blue T-shirt, and brushed her hair into a ponytail. She glanced at the clock on her nightstand. It was late, her parents had probably already had their breakfast. She shrugged. That was OK. All she wanted was a piece of toast and a glass of juice. The feeling that something good was about to happen flickered in her mind, and it was too strong a feeling to ignore. Was it because she had finally reached a decision?

The house seemed exceptionally quiet. On the kitchen table she found a note from her mother propped against the sugar bowl.

Bobbie scanned the hastily written message.

Aunt Ida called from Niagara Falls. She's getting ready to move to a smaller house and wondered if we could give her a hand packing family pictures and dishes. It sounds boring, so we didn't think you'd want to come along. We should be home before dark.

Bobbie put an English muffin in the toaster and poured a glass of orange juice. Her mother was right. Sorting through boxes of old things didn't sound very exciting. She would rather stay home than go and listen to Aunt Ida complain about her aches and pains and the high cost of living.

Bobbie stared out the back window, where a pair of gray squirrels played a game of tag under the trees. It was definitely the weather for spring fever. If Nancy hadn't gone away with Bill and his parents for the day, they could go for a nice long bike ride to the lake.

Bobbie turned away from the window, feeling suddenly lonely. It was too nice a day to waste. Maybe if she phoned George he'd want to go to a movie. No, she knew better. George would only want to see a science fiction film. If there wasn't one playing at a theater, he'd rent a tape for the VCR. That day she was in the mood for a snappy comedy, something to make her laugh and forget about facing Mrs. Trumble the next day, not a creepy super fly or a man from Mars. She looked out her window again. What was wrong with her, anyway? Why had her earlier premonition of something good happening vanished? She had her decision firmly set in her mind. She should feel a lot happier about it than she did. All right, enough gloom. She didn't want to spend an entire day moping, that was for sure. She reached for the phone. Maybe Ellen and Amy would want to go to the zoo or something. She picked up the phone and dialed her sister's number.

Disappointed when no one answered after several rings, Bobbie took a box of cookies from the cupboard and nibbled one. She vaguely remembered that Ellen had mentioned taking Amy to visit a friend with a new baby. It looked as if she would be on her own, like it or not. She turned again to the window. The gray squirrels had vanished. Even the birds' songs had stopped. She glanced at the phone longingly. Wouldn't it be great if Jay phoned right that minute? A picture of his face flashed into her mind, and suddenly she could see

why she had lost her temper and said she
never wanted to see him again. She had been
hurt and diappointed. Jay should have known
she didn't really mean it. She sighed, shaking her head. She wanted very much to see
Jay again, to have him back in her life. If he
had to spend most of his time with banjo
lessons, she would be happy to see him once
a week, or once a month. She just wanted to
be able to talk to him again.

Her thoughts were interrupted by the ringing of the phone. She felt a slight flutter in
the pit of her stomach. It couldn't be Jay.
That was a dream that would never come
true.

"Hello."

"Bobbie? It's Miss Tillis at Lakeside Nursing Home. Remember I called a while ago to
say we might want you to perform? We need
you now, desperately. We've decided to give
Mrs. Dombroski her birthday party today while
she's feeling up to it. She's ninety-five, and
we would like to do something special. I know
it's short notice, but we couldn't plan anything earlier. Poor Mrs. Dombroski had a bad
case of bronchitis and wasn't up to the excitement of a party until today. Please say
you can come." Her voice was pleading.

Bobbie remembered the frail birdlike woman
with snapping black eyes and hair the color

of new-fallen snow. She loved to play bingo and show off the prizes she had won. Bobbie smiled, remembering the way the woman entered into sing-alongs and laughed at Bubbles.

For a moment Bobbie stared thoughtfully at the phone. One more appearance wouldn't hurt—one final farewell show for Mrs. Dombroski. She had nothing better to do that day. "Sure, I'll be glad to come," she said. "But, I'll need a ride."

"That will be no problem," Miss Tillis said, sounding relieved. "I'll pick you up myself at one-thirty sharp."

"I'll be ready," Bobbie assured her. And she scrambled to gather her props, apply her makeup, and dress in her clown outfit before Miss Tillis came for her.

A short time later when they arrived at the nursing home, the parking lot was already packed with cars.

"This is a big occasion," Miss Tillis told her, a faint smile on her pale lips. "We think ninety-five years on this earth deserves a party. A reporter from the *Daily Herald* will be there." Her smile widened. "Mrs. Dombroski will be a star today."

Bobbie thought about it as she hurried to the quiet lounge to give her makeup a final check. She hummed, as she patted more white

139

powder on her forehead, then paused to stare at her green-haired reflection in the mirror. There was something different about Bubbles today. Was her smile wider than usual? Had she painted more freckles on her nose? She shrugged. Everything seemed the same as usual. Her stomach churned, but that, too, was normal. It wasn't, she remembered, the feeling she'd had earlier that day—the "something good is about to happen" feeling. Maybe this appearance was what her premonition was about.

Bobbie stood in the hall outside the recreation room, waiting until it was her turn to entertain. She listened while an elderly man played a few familiar old songs on a battered old accordion. Guests and patients joined him in singing the last song. Bobbie hummed along, tapping her big shoe in time to the music. When he left the stage, a plump, red-faced woman wearing a lavender chiffon dress sang an opera number. Bobbie watched her get redder and redder with each high note, and giggled when the woman waved her arms. The chiffon fluttered like a giant moth's wings. But her voice wasn't bad, and everyone liked her. At least they were polite and clapped, and she bowed again and again.

Then it was time for Bubbles to make her entrance. As usual, once she stumbled into the room and headed for the stage she forgot Bobbie Reese completely. Ceremoniously, she spread papers on the stage and proceeded to attempt a juggling act using four tomatoes. The result was disastrous, and the room rocked with applause and laughter.

Bobbie was onstage for several minutes before she glanced around the audience. That was when she saw Jay. Her heart pounded, and for a brief instant she stood rooted to the center of the stage, staring. Jay was sitting next to an elderly man in a wheelchair, and when she looked at him, Jay's eyes met hers. He stared at her for a moment, then she saw his hand raise and give her the A-OK sign. Bobbie suddenly felt on top of the world. She went back into the act with renewed energy, doing a clumsy waltz with a mop borrowed from the janitor who watched from the doorway. It was so good to see Jay again, even if it was just a brief glimpse in a crowded room. And his gesture had proved to her that he was no longer angry. She finished her act feeling better than she had in a long time. On her way out, she paused to give Mrs. Dombroski a hug. The old lady squeezed her hand and whispered, "Thank you for making my birthday special. I love Bubbles. And I love the dear girl underneath the makeup."

Bobbie kissed the woman's wrinkled cheek, and someone nearby snapped a picture.

She made her way to the lounge, pausing now and then to accept congratulations from visitors and patients for a job well done. She felt warm and good, certain the act had been better than usual. The response from the elderly patients told her how much they enjoyed Bubbles; and strangely enough, for the first time, she felt she owed Jay special thanks. She could see now that it was possible he had done her a favor when he had left the act. Jay had had more faith in her going on with Bubbles alone than she had. If she saw him again, she would tell him.

No one was in the lounge when she hurriedly removed her makeup and transformed herself back into Bobbie Reese. She picked up the suitcase containing the costume and her props and went down the hall toward the office to wait for her ride home. She walked, head down, thinking of Jay sitting in the audience, watching her perform. He looked terrific. His hair was still on the long side, but his smile was the same. Fantastic. At the end of the hall, she turned to go down the short corridor to the office and bumped into someone coming the other way. She struggled to hang on to her suitcase and maintain her balance, but her suitcase dropped, sliding across the polished floor. A pair of strong hands reached out to steady her.

"Nice going," said a familiar voice.

She glanced up, looking directly into Jay's indigo-blue eyes, and her heart did a flip. "Nothing has changed," she told him, smiling. "I'm as clumsy as ever—with or without the clown suit."

He looked at her for a long moment before taking her hands in his and holding them tightly. "Some things never change," he said. "How have you been, Bobbie? You look terrific."

She had no intention of telling him how miserable she had been since their Valentine's Day breakup. "I'm fine," she told him with a shrug. "How about you?" Actually, even if the feeling didn't last, and Jay left to go home to his banjo, right then she was on top of the world. He was speaking to her as if nothing had happened between them. "What are you doing here?" she asked him. "I was surprised to see you out in the audience."

"I came to see our neighbor. He had a slight stroke last month, and he's here until he gets back on his feet. He's alone, so my folks and I take turns visiting him," Jay explained. "I wasn't sure if you were still doing the act. I was really surprised to see Bubbles bound onto the stage."

Bobbie giggled. "Bound? There is no way

Bubbles could bound onto anything in those size-twenty shoes. Are you sure you saw the act?"

He released her hands and stood looking down at her, his expression serious. "You saw me out in the audience watching you. You were great. I told you you could do it, Bobbie. You never needed anyone to lead you onstage. I'd say you've grown up a bit since our breakup."

"How?" she asked him curiously.

He shrugged. "It's hard to explain. You just seem more sure of yourself."

"What about you?" she asked quietly. "How are the banjo lessons coming along?" It was strange. She was no longer resentful of his music. In fact, she found she was actually interested.

He sighed. "It's a long story, Bobbie. I think we have to talk about it. Why don't we cut out of this place and go for a walk. The lake should be peaceful today." He grinned at her. "We can skip a few stones."

"Miss Tillis, the recreation director, is going to drive me home," she said, watching Jay's face for a reaction.

He took her arm and propelled her toward the office. "Tell her you have a ride home," he said. "A lot of things have happened to me. I want to tell you everything. I owe you that much."

Suddenly Bobbie remembered the day she and George had gone to the Noise Box and had seen Jay come in and go straight to a table in the back to sit with a very pretty girl. Was that what he wanted to tell her, that he had found someone else? Her stomach churned. Did she really want to know? At least, until this moment, she had her hopes and dreams. The next few minutes could erase those dreams forever. She looked away from Jay, staring at a row of paintings done by patients that lined the wall outside the recreation office.

Jay glanced at her, puzzled. "Hey, why so glum? We're going for a walk on the beach. Go on in and tell Miss Tillis you won't need a ride because you've had another offer. Come on, I want to skip those stones." He gave her a smile. "And I want to talk. We have to."

Chapter Thirteen

The walk to the shore of the lake was short. The sun glistened on the water, and gentle waves rolled onto the beach. A slight breeze tugged at Bobbie's hair as she and Jay walked along the water's edge. Now and then Jay paused to pick up a flat stone and send it bouncing over the water. Each time he counted the skips.

"I never could get more than four," he muttered. "How about you? I'll bet you can't get one skip."

Bobbie laughed. "I'll have you know I usually get five."

Jay's eyes widened in surprise. "You're kidding." He picked up another stone and tossed it. "I'll have to do better this time."

Bobbie kept careful count. "One, two—three. You're getting worse," she informed him cheerfully.

"You think you're pretty smart, don't you?" he said, grinning at her. "Of course, how do I know you really scored five? You're going to have to prove it."

"You asked for it." Bobbie searched the sand for just the right size stone, smooth and oval, just as her father had shown her years ago, and sent it skimming over the water.

Jay counted the skips. "Five," he moaned. "I've been outskimmed by a clown!"

They laughed, and any remaining tension between them vanished. Jay pointed to a big log a short distance ahead, and they sat down on it, watching a pair of sea gulls search the shore for food.

Finally Jay spoke, his voice husky with emotion. "It's been a long time since we talked, Bobbie. A lot has happened in my life."

Bobbie felt herself stiffen. Did she really want to hear this? He went on, and she had no choice but to listen.

"For starters, the night of the Valentine's Day dance, when you said you never wanted to see me again, I was sure you meant it. I knew I'd hurt you, and I hated myself for it. I figured you must hate me, too," he told her. "It took me a long time to adjust to not seeing

148

you at all, or even phoning." He paused. "I wanted to talk to you, to try to make you understand how I feel about my banjo lessons, Bobbie. I've done more practicing lately that I've ever done before." He gave her a crooked little smile. "I wanted to ask you to a dance we had at school a few weeks ago, but so much time had gone by, I didn't think I should butt into your life. Once, right after we broke up, I tried to phone but when no one answered I gave up." He kicked absently at a piece of driftwood. "Chickened out is more like it. I had to put our good times out of my mind and go on with my life. My lessons with Milken were great, and they meant a lot to me. I practiced every minute I had free. I didn't have any time for anything except school and banjo."

Bobbie leaned down, letting her fingers trace a circle in the sand. "I saw you one day, when George and I stopped at a little restaurant near the library, and you came in."

He looked puzzled. "The Noise Box? I didn't see you. Why didn't you say something?"

She watched a sea gull sweep low and plunge into the water to grab a fish. "You seemed occupied," she told him quietly. "You headed toward a back table to meet someone." She wasn't going to mention that she had seen the pretty dark-haired girl waiting for him.

"Oh," he said, remembering. "That was the day I wanted to celebrate because I had finished my last banjo lesson."

Bobbie took a deep breath. Now he was going to tell her he'd asked another girl to his dance and they were in love. And she would have to tell him she was glad for him and pretend that it didn't matter. She shook her head. There was no way she could do that. Seeing Jay again, sitting there next to him on the quiet beach, made her realize just how much he meant to her. She hadn't been able to put him out of her mind since that unhappy Valentine's Day.

Jay leaned down to watch her drawing in the sand. "As I said, Bobbie, I wanted to celebrate. I felt like having a hot-fudge sundae, so I asked my cousin Jill to meet me. She works in the library after school."

Bobbie concentrated on drawing a smiling face on her circle. She couldn't look at Jay now. She might do something stupid, like cry. She wanted to believe him, but she didn't care. "You never mentioned that you had a cousin Jill." She drew an upside-down mouth on a second sand face.

"It never came up. I don't know how many cousins you have, either."

Bobbie continued her drawing, adding curly hair and a stick-figure body.

Jay moaned. "Bobbie, will you sit up and look at me. Trying to explain things to you is like talking to this log we're sitting on."

Reluctantly Bobbie sat up, facing him. "Sorry. I happen to like sand doodles."

"Why doesn't that surprise me?" he teased. "The Bobbie Reese I know and love enjoys doing weird things." He reached out, looking straight into her eyes, and brushed a lock of hair from her face.

Bobbie felt a warm glow spread over her. Had she heard him correctly? Had he really said the word love? The look in his eyes told her she hadn't been mistaken, and his next words confirmed it. "I missed you, Bobbie. And I missed all the fun we had together. I've never known anyone quite like you, you know. There's a lot of Bobbie Reese in Bubbles whether she admits it or not. That's what makes that clown so special."

Bobbie brushed sand from her fingers. "There's something you don't know, Jay. I'm giving up the act and retiring Bubbles to the trunk in the attic. This was my last performance."

He pulled back, looking surprised. "Why? I hear the act is in demand."

She nodded. "It is. I have a lot of requests

to do parties and hospital shows. But, Jay, I've been offered a job in the school office." She drew in a deep breath. "Sometimes clowning is depressing. It isn't as much fun as it was when we entertained together. Sometimes it's so sad seeing all those sick people." She shivered and told him about the critically ill heart patient.

He nodded, his expression sympathetic. "I've faced that," he told her gently. "Now, I have two important questions to ask you. Did the patient enjoy Bubbles? Did she respond?"

Bobbie was thoughtful. "She took my hand and smiled."

"How did that make you feel?" Jay asked, studying her face.

"Good—kind of warm inside. I guess for a few minutes I felt special, as if I had done something helpful. It's hard to explain."

"Isn't that the answer to your dilemma?" he asked, his voice a soothing murmur. "Isn't that what being a clown is all about?"

Bobbie nodded. "Giving enjoyment and feeling good about it." She knew exactly what Jay meant. "You're right," she said. "If I continue the act, I'll be a lot happier than I would be working in a stuffy office." She turned to face him. "Thanks, partner. I feel as though a cloud that's been hanging over my head has suddenly blown away. Of course, going onstage isn't the same without you, but I proved I can do it alone."

"You sure did," he said, "and you'll go on. You're too good to quit. By the way, since my lessons with my special teacher have ended, I have a free hour or two now and then—enough time to make a guest appearance or two and date my special girl."

When she looked at him questioningly he gave her an infectious grin. "That's you, in case you're wondering."

She threw her arms around his neck and hugged him. "I was hoping," she exclaimed happily.

"Come here." Jay drew her close. His kiss was warm and gentle and sent a tingle up her spine. When it was over she sat a moment, still feeling it, then bent down to remove her shoes.

"Now what?" he asked.

She jumped up from the log and whirled around in circles before running along the shore, in and out of the water, doing crazy Bubbles-type antics. "I'm Bubbles and I chase troubles," she shouted as she ran.

Jay quickly removed his own shoes and dashed after her, shouting, "You're something else, that's what you are!"

She laughed, calling back, "I know. Isn't it terrific?"

He caught up to her and grabbed her hand in his. They walked along the beach silently for a while, just enjoying the feel of the cool sand squishing between their toes and the cries of the sea gulls circling overhead. Now and then a gentle wave rolled in, covering their feet in cold foam. Neither Bobbie nor Jay noticed. His arm slipped around her waist as they walked. The sun on the water was dazzling, and their futures seemed just as bright.